PENGUIN BO

HAZELL

Terry Venables and Gordon ~~~~~~~~~~~ 50s
when Terry Venables was captain of Chelsea and
Gordon Williams, then a freelance journalist, was asked
to run the team's business activities. Their first join ven-
ture was a football novel, *They Used to Play on Grass*
(to be reissued by Penguin in 1995), before going on to
write the crime novels *Hazell Plays Solomon*, *Hazell and
the Three-Card Trick* and *Hazell and the Menacing
Jester*. James Hazell, the London private detective at the
centre of these books, was also the basis for the popular
television series made in the late 1970s.

Terry Venables, the current coach of the England football team, has the unique distinction of having been
capped by England at every level in football, from
schoolboy to full international. He joined Chelsea at the
age of fifteen and has played for (and managed) Queen's
Park Rangers, Spurs and Crystal Palace. In addition to
his successful football career both on and off the pitch,
he is known as an author, singer, television personality
and businessman. His *Autobiography* was recently published by Michael Joseph.

Gordon Williams was born in Paisley and after RAF
service spent several years as a journalist. He is the
author of many books including *Straw Dogs*, *Big Morning Blues*, *Walk Don't Walk* and *From Scenes Like
These* (which was shortlisted for the Booker Prize). He is
also a screenwriter. The 'Hazell' books, worked on
when Venables had finished daily training at QPR, were
originally published under the combined pseudonym
P. B. Yuill.

Terry Venables and
Gordon Williams

Hazell Plays Solomon

PENGUIN BOOKS

PENGUIN BOOKS

Published by the Penguin Group
Penguin Books Ltd, 27 Wrights Lane, London W8 5TZ, England
Penguin Books USA Inc., 375 Hudson Street, New York, New York 10014, USA
Penguin Books Australia Ltd, Ringwood, Victoria, Australia
Penguin Books Canada Ltd, 10 Alcorn Avenue, Toronto, Ontario, Canada M4V 3B2
Penguin Books (NZ) Ltd, 182–190 Wairau Road, Auckland 10, New Zealand

Penguin Books Ltd, Registered Offices: Harmondsworth, Middlesex, England

First published by Macmillan 1974
Published in Penguin Books 1976
10 9 8 7 6 5 4

Originally published under the pseudonym P. B. Yuill

Printed in England by Clays Ltd, St Ives plc
Set in Linotype Pilgrim

Chapter One

My name is James Hazell and I'm the biggest bastard who ever pushed your bell-button.

No, that wasn't how I introduced myself to the creepy Clifford Abrey but it should have been, that warm July evening in the east end of London Town.

I had just given my newly-healed ankle a punishing work-out on seven flights of concrete stairs in a grey barrack block of flats called Herbert Morrison House in tatty old Bethnal Green.

If Abrey had known the truth about my visit he would have chucked me down the shaft of the wonky lift. Or at least he would have tried.

But I didn't know myself, not then. If I had I would have done a quick disappearing act from the whole deal.

Baby capers are not my line . . .

Before I climbed that dump in the sky I had a drive round the district, just for old times' sake. I wasn't brought up in Bethnal Green but not too far away.

For all the changes the cemetery was still the area showpiece, the one place where the poor finally get a fair share of something.

Herbert Morrison House was a twenty-storey block, shabby and rain-streaked, the walls thick with spray-can messages, nicknames, gang slogans, incurable optimism about West Ham football team. I parked the car across the street, hoping the Abreys' flat would have a window on that side. It was a new navy blue, two door Triumph Stag which I had owned for two whole days. I'd chosen it with places like this in mind, where a flash job attracts every eager hand in the borough. The Stag could pass for ordinary – until you tried to pass it.

It took me a good ten minutes to climb those seven flights. It was only a month since they'd removed the last lot of plaster from my dud ankle and not much longer since I'd stopped trying to drink myself into the happy communism of the graveyard.

That ankle! It had been done eighteen months before, when some reluctant clients in Fulham had slammed a car door on it three or four times.

Since then it had been broken and re-set twice by cheerful doctors.

That bloody ankle! It cost me my career, my marriage and almost did for my sanity. I would have had it amputated only I was too attached to my right foot . . .

I had to take a couple of minutes' rest on the fifth floor landing. Were they hoping to let the top flats to our Olympic team? I was certainly suffering. When you get to my age fitness isn't a happy accident, it's a daily grind and I don't mean the kind that cures acne.

On the seventh floor I took a couple of deep breaths to remind my lungs who was supposed to be guvnor.

Limping slightly I found the door I was looking for, Number 57, white plastic numerals on smart green paint, the smartest door I'd seen in that shabby sky-tunnel.

I put my thumb on the button.

I was wearing a dove-grey suede jacket, three-quarter length, over a white rollneck sweater and fawn summer strides. This was supposed to be casual gear but as I heard footsteps vibrating behind the door I was beginning to feel almost elegant. Herbert Morrison House was by no means the business, even by Bethnal Green standards.

A man opened the door. He had short black hair that hung down to his eyebrows in a greasy, unintentional fringe. He was wearing a white nylon shirt, vest showing through, dark grey flannels and brown slippers. His face was pale and he wasn't smiling.

'Good evening,' I said. 'Mr Abrey? My name's James Hazell.'

I smiled. He nodded. At least his Hitler-style fringe shook a little.

'Sorry to bother you,' I said, 'I wonder if you can spare me a few moments – it's about St Margaret's Hospital, I believe your wife had a – '

Before my casual openers were finished he looked over his shoulder and shouted:

'Toni?'

Only he said it Townee.

I saw straight away he was a man for quick decisions.

Then Mrs Toni Abrey came to his side.

I tried not to let my surprise show.

She was a blonde sort, middle twenties, straight fair hair just long enough to cover her ears. Her blue eyes gave me the once-over.

In this line of work I always find that first impressions are the best. They are usually wrong but I try to look on the bright side. And the kind of people you deal with in this racket tend to deteriorate under close examination.

Toni Abrey knocked me over from that very first moment, from her dyed blonde crop to her wedge-heel pom-poms. Her blue eyes seemed to shine out of her face and she was built for action.

What the hell was she doing married to this dum-dum? After those stairs I knew it wasn't his seat on the stock exchange and he didn't look like a bundle of laughs.

Unless, as we used to say in the East End, this was only a front and there was a dry-cleaner's at the back.

'I was just explaining to your husband – my name's James Hazell,' I said, 'are you the Mrs Abrey who had a baby in St Margaret's Hospital about five years ago?'

'Six years next month,' she said. Her eyes never left mine.

'A mother's memory, eh' I smiled, although she didn't look the type to go in for baby slush. 'I'm doing some research into St Margaret's maternity section.'

'What kind of research?' she asked, quickly but with no nervousness.

If possible, I had vowed to myself, I would never tell an out-right lie again. Looking back, my past life seemed to have been either a million little lies – or maybe just one big lie.

Not that I worried about my teeth turning black; if pushed I could give truth the elbow quicker than a cabinet minister. But I was making a fresh start and I was determined not to create a fresh mess. What is a lie anyway but laziness?

Today's lie is tomorrow's trouble, said a great philosopher called James Hazell.

If life was all down to theory I'd be king.

'I suppose you've seen the show,' I said, mentioning a well-known TV documentary series. 'I'm doing background research.'

I was talking – or lying – exclusively to her by then. He didn't seem to carry a lot of weight in those parts.

I wasn't too sure if she believed me but after a moment she asked me in. He closed the door behind us. He followed me and I followed her solid buttocks.

Their living-room wasn't much larger than a telephone box. It was dominated by a colour television which neither of them bothered to turn off, although she did lower the sound.

On top of the TV set was a round glass bowl. It contained a couple of pints of cloudy water and one small goldfish swimming frantically in circles as if excited by the presence of a new face. The walls were papered in an insipid, light-brown pattern, a background that suited him but not her, I thought, trying hard not to be caught clocking her bristols which were covered, you could call it, by Marks and Sparks's latest creation in white man-made.

'How long have you had the fish?' I asked, peering down into murky water.

'We got it Saturday morning, down the market,' said Clifford Abrey apologetically, 'only a couple of bob, it's for Trish really.'

'This'll be Trish, is it?' I asked, picking up a mounted photograph beside the fish bowl, one of those cheap hand-coloured jobs that make your best friend seem only vaguely familiar, if you have that class of friend.

The child had red hair – even those satirical tints that turn everybody's face into a bowl of strawberries and cream couldn't disguise the colour – but as a portrait it put Identikits in the Rembrandt class.

If this was the best photo they had we would have to snatch a picture of the kid in the street.

'You're overfeeding the fish,' I said, putting down the photo-case. 'All that gunge at the bottom is what kills them. Feed once a day with a very light hand, that's the secret.' I smiled apologetically. Abrey's style was infectious. 'My landlord is a fish nut,' I said.

'We only bought it for Trish, dint we, Toni?' he said.

She was not over-impressed by my subtle use of fish diets to break the ice but she pointed to the couch, which was a dingy orange colour. I sat down, unable to hide a slight wince as I gave the wonky ankle a rub.

'There's talk of 'em knocking St Margaret's down,' he said, standing indecisively in front of the mock-log electric fire. 'Is it to do with that?'

She sat opposite me in one of the two easy chairs. You might have thought that particular shade of orange was a dyer's experiment gone wrong but no – it was intentional and there was a matching three-piece suite to prove it.

She crossed her legs. Even under her emerald green trousers I could tell she had good knees. I was glad they were covered by the trousers. I had enough not to be staring at them furtively as it was.

'You mind if I smoke?' I brought out a packet of those French Gauloises. Gordon Gregory put me on to that brand. He said there was very little lung cancer in France. It was the healthy way to smoke yourself to death, he said.

An ashtray large enough to hold three buttons at a squeeze was placed at my elbow. Neither of them smoked but he was kind enough to remove the three buttons.

'I've seen your programme mentioned in the papers,' he said. 'I don't think we've ever actually watched it, have we, Toni?'

'Oh no, we're a commercial family,' she said. I looked quickly but if she was being sarcastic he hadn't noticed.

'I got your names from hospital records,' I said. That wasn't a lie. 'The idea is to do something about these old Victorian hospitals – what people feel about them, should they be torn down, you know the sort of thing.'

'It was under-staffed, we did notice that, didn't we Toni?' said you know who.

She was no dum-dum. Most of the door-to-door sharks were still using the old market research gimmick. She was expecting me to launch into a sales spiel for handwoven encyclopedias or wall-to-wall insurance schemes.

It was then we heard the sirens.

Abrey was out of that room like trap number four. Just for a moment she and I were alone.

'No, I'm not flogging anything,' I said.

'Got your word on that, have I?'

'Straight.'

She smiled.

We understood each other *perfectly*.

Of course, if I had known then what the job was all about I would have kept my eyes glued to the hideous orange upholstery. But I had been told by Gordon Gregory that it was only a simple tracing operation. And it isn't often the trail leads to someone like her.

In fact my trail hadn't led me *anywhere* for nearly three months.

We heard Abrey shouting so we went through a small bedroom to reach the balcony. The bed hadn't been made. He pointed.

Two blue and white squad cars were speeding up Sutherland Avenue, the main street outside the block. Uniformed flatties were already erupting from the cars as they bumped onto the cleared building site on one side of Herbert's house.

Down below us fifty or sixty boys and youths, black and white, had been having a ruck in the fenced-off playground. They stopped booting and knuckling each other when they saw Old Bill.

I leaned out as far as gravity allowed but could not see my precious new Stag.

The flower of East End youth broke ranks in a mass stampede through a hole in the wire-mesh fence that was supposed to keep the little playground safe for the under-sevens. Just for a moment it had seemed likely the two teams of bother boys might stand their ground. There were a lot of them and only seven coppers.

But they ran and we could hear their shouts and jeers as they rampaged across the cleared site, streams of lads flowing round rusting car-carcasses and broken prams and dumped mattresses and all the other valuable specimens that archaeologists would breathe heavily over next century.

'Bleeding animals,' Abrey growled, 'I'd chase 'em back up their bloody banana trees, no messing.'

I'd just been thinking it was a reassuring sign, black and white being mixed, I mean. For a moment I had the impression I was seeing a different Clifford Abrey.

Old Bill gave up the chase half-way across the building site. They came back to the cars, taking off flat caps to wipe foreheads. It was a very hot night. The scent coming off Toni Abrey beside me on the balcony wasn't making me any cooler.

One of the patrol cars drove down Sutherland Avenue. From the open windows of the other car we could hear the fuzzy boom of radio voices.

Four or five years ago it might have been me down there, I thought, without too much regret.

Then the second car moved off into the early twilight, its blue roof-light blinking under the orange sodiums of the street.

'You wonder why I don't fancy Trish being left down there on her own?' Abrey said as we went back into the living-room.

'It's too rough for our little princess,' she said to me. This time there was no mistaking the sarcasm.

'The council wants to mend that bleeding fence and supervise properly,' he said. We sat down again in a sea of orange.

'It won't be done till some kid gets hurt by them tearaways,' she said. 'Why don't you go down to the council offices and kick up a stink?'

'Yeah I would,' he said, 'only I'd have to take time off work, wouldn't I?'

'One cert, you can't keep her in cottonwool all her life,' she said.

'I'll just see if she's all right.'

'Could I have a look at your little girl?' I asked, with what I hoped was the right kind of gooey expression.

'Sure,' said Abrey, one of the few occasions he didn't wait for his wife's say-so. I was beginning to get a pretty clear picture of the Abrey set-up.

Like the rest of the flat – small, cluttered rooms, colours either faded or too bright, and always clashing – the child's bedroom was just this side of a mess.

My feet searched for landing-space among a spread of plastic toys, the cheap kind, mass-produced in Hong Kong and guaranteed to hold together until the cash register stops pinging.

Patricia Abrey, aged six, was twisted half out of the blankets, lying across her pillow. With the curtains drawn I could just tell that her hair was red.

Above the bed, stuck to the wall with four pins, was a colour print of Jesus, torn from a magazine. That year most kids were pinning up boy canaries with Lolita faces. I had a pretty shrewd idea that it was Cliff Abrey who belonged to the Lord's fan club.

Murmuring cosily, he lifted her back into place and bent down to kiss her forehead.

'Pretty, isn't she?' he said, with no trace of modesty.

I nodded. Gordon Gregory wasn't paying me enough for that kind of slush. It's my deficiency, I know, but anything under nineteen leaves me cold. Not many over nineteens do much for me either, unless they're female.

'She gets the red hair from her Gran,' he explained as if I had been dying to know. 'We was Irish originally.'

We went back into the living-room. On the TV screen I saw Natalie Wood running down a lawn in front of a large, white house. Suntanned children were splashing in a blue pool, screaming dialogue at each other in American accents.

'Cor, what a smashing place,' Abrey said. 'That would do us nicely, eh, Toni?'

'When we win the pools,' she snorted, standing up. 'Could you go a lager and lime or something?' she asked me.

'No thanks.'

'I think there's a drop of scotch left.'

'No thanks, I don't.'

'Go on, you look the thirsty type.'

'I have no vices.'

'None?'

'Only telling lies.'

She smiled down at me. I smiled back. Abrey watched the TV. She didn't take long to produce the tea, in Woolworth's cups. While she was out of the room Abrey gave me a couple of guilty smiles but had nothing to say.

For some reason I couldn't take my eyes off that greasy fringe of his. It was enough to bring back crewcuts.

The tea was rotten. All in all nobody was going to put Toni Abrey in for Housewife of the Year.

'What do you want me to tell you about the hospital?' she asked.

'Anything that comes to mind. Any complaints?'

'It was clean enough.' She shrugged. Presumably she believed my story now but she wasn't coming out in a lather about the chance of a TV appearance. I liked that. I also liked the fact that housework obviously bored the pants off her.

I wondered if I could do likewise.

It was just a thought.

'Do we get paid for helping you?' she asked briskly.

'Well, it sort of depends on –'

'We ain't looking to be paid,' he said, embarrassedly.

'Why the hell not?' she snapped. 'We too rich to need it, are we?' She looked at me, 'I only want to know. Cliff's been on short-time at the factory and this week they're on strike – he thinks on six quid a week strike pay we're too proud to ask for money!' She turned on him. 'Who was making all the fuss about Tricia not going on that outing with the school to Cromer cos we couldn't afford a lousy pound?'

'Yeah,' he said, apologetically, 'we're on strike cos they've only been giving us a half-week –'

'You know bloody well that colour set's going back to the rental firm if your Mum won't give us twenty quid,' she said.

'If we go-ahead and you're one of the families we use you would get paid something,' I said, 'but don't book any Mediterranean holidays at this stage.'

'Holidays?' she snorted. 'We had a week in a leaky caravan in Devon two year ago! And that was only because your Mum paid – which meant she was bloody well with us!' She turned to

13

me again, forcing a smile. 'We got to have a colour set and a car, mind, so we're struggling to pay for the absolute luxuries before we can get the necessities.'

I smiled back.

'So what can you remember about the hospital?' I said.

'The nurses and doctors was all right – a bit off hand but they're worked so hard – '

'What about that old witch who had all the barneys?' he chipped in, only too glad we were off the money question.

'Oh yeah – Drummond – a right old dragon she was. The woman in the next bed to me, she had some right up-and-downers with her. She had me a bit scared, tell the truth.'

'She had me nervous and I was only visiting,' said Abrey, smiling at the nonsensical idea he could be scared of anything.

'Really, he ought to have the babies, he panics enough,' she said. 'First time he come to visit me he bumps into that Georgina's husband – couldn't see where he was going for flowers.' She grimaced. 'Never had so much as a bunch of daffodils since.'

'Toni and that Georgina both had girls on the same day,' he said, looking at me to marvel.

I nodded in appreciation of this double miracle.

'She lives about here as it happens,' Toni said.

'Who does?' he asked, frowning.

'Old Drummond, of course! I keep seeing her in the street, least I used to. Down Whitnell Street way I think.'

'Funny place for a nurse to live, innit? Sure she weren't just visiting?'

'I don't know, do I?' she snapped.

I made some notes, mainly to give my face something to do while they were squawking at each other. I asked a few questions. He was a semi-skilled machinist who at best earned about £28 a week. He had other views besides his colour prejudice. He didn't really believe in trade unions and had only joined the strike because scabbing meant you would probably never work again.

Broke as they were he wouldn't lower the family tone by letting her go out to work.

He had been brought up a Catholic but wasn't, he said, 'as

regular' as he ought to be. I got the impression they had rows about whether the little girl should go to Mass.

It wasn't a hard impression to get. They had a row in front of me. She thought religion was a lot of cobblers, he couldn't even mention God without a quick look over his shoulder.

The surprising thing about him was his age. I would have said late thirties, possibly older, but in fact he was the same age as myself. He certainly seemed a lot older than thirty-three.

She was twenty-eight. They weren't going to have any more children, he said. It was hard enough bringing up Trish on his wages and he didn't believe in taking all the overtime going. She didn't seem to care.

'Them others at the factory take all the hours they can get when the shop is busy 'cos they're not interested in their family life,' he explained earnestly. 'I mean, you got a kid, she needs her parents, that's what's causing all this hooliganism and delinquency, innit, it's down to the parents, that's what I always say, isn't it, Toni?'

'He's a snob,' she said to me, 'he don't even believe in letting her play with the rest of the kids in this block in case she picks up rough ways.'

He regarded this as a family joke. At least it made him grin.

I got to my feet.

'I've often said our Trish would be the ideal sort for the telly,' he said, 'she's ten times prettier than most of them kids they get on the commercials, I've said that often, haven't I, Toni?'

'Mr Hazell works for the BBC,' she said coldly.

'Just as a freelance,' I said, 'I mean, I'll work for anybody who pays me. This one is my own idea, so let's hope they like it.'

Then I did something that seemed a bit trivial at the time. I fished out one of my cards, brand new, artificially formal, just my name and Dot Wilmington's phone number.

'There may be something else you remember,' I said, hesitating, the card between my fingers.

She reached out and took it.

Which was the vague idea I'd had when I got the card out in the first place.

As she was closing the door behind me she gave me a look. Nothing dramatic – but a look, all the same. The card was still in her hand.

'Remember about the fish,' I said.

'Oh yeah.' Her blue eyes stared at me. 'Once a day and lightly, that's your motto, isn't it?'

The door closed.

It was easier going down.

No, I wouldn't see her again, I told myself.

As I turned from the third floor landing I bumped into somebody.

There were two of them, big lads, both black. The one I had knocked into was leaning against the wall. The other was a few steps down.

'Sorry,' I said.

They were both wearing narrow-brimmed hats, several sizes too small. They could have been from the mob the cops broke up. Neither of them spoke.

'You should look where I'm going,' I quipped. They just stared at me.

I passed the first one. The second made no move to get out of my way. Their faces were impenetrable.

I had the urge. Bang their heads against the wall, on principle.

But that was something else I had put behind me.

I sidestepped the second one and went on down, taking care not to show any suggestion of a limp. At the next landing I looked back up. They hadn't moved, just two big lads going nowhere and waiting for someone to tell them to go somewhere else.

I knew exactly how they felt. I always did, even when I *was* banging heads against walls.

Maybe I was improving.

As I crossed the street towards the car I was looking for the signs that tell you somebody's been tampering, the little signs – like no engine or four missing wheels. It seemed okay.

Fiddling absent-mindedly with my bunch of twirls I stared up at the windows of Herbert's house. I couldn't tell which balcony we'd looked down from but it made me think curious thoughts, knowing that Toni Abrey was up in that high-rise monstrosity, going through the motions of a life.

Maybe I would see her again, if I happened to be just passing the seventh floor of Herbert Morrison House on some footling errand.

As I started the car and headed west for the City I wondered why a client in Los Angeles would be interested in the Abreys.

Half an hour later I was letting myself into the big, empty house in Putney, feeling tired but knowing I had those bleeding fish to tuck in. I was thinking it might be easier to pay an extortionate rent (if there's any other kind left) than get free lodgings for looking after twelve gurgling tanks of Rag Trade Reggie's tropicals.

The free digs were something else I owed to Gordon Gregory. Apart from my new career, I mean.

Rag Trade Reggie, being called away unexpectedly for twelve years less good conduct remission, needed somebody to look after his collection of exotic tiddlers. Seemingly at his last meeting with Gordon, in the cells under the court, he'd been more worried about them than about his wife and family.

I had moved in, as wet-nurse, until he could arrange to sell the lot. He was master-minding this operation from his new administrative suite on the Isle of Wight.

He had lived in luxury, Rag Trade Reggie Mancini, a master of the long-firm swindle by day and a tropical fish lunatic by night.

With thousands homeless in London Town that smooth old villain could afford to devote two large rooms in his big Putney house to fish tanks – marine tropicals from the Pacific, veiltail angels, two pairs of giant Discus, vicious Paradise pintails, giant Oscars, hatchings of some new swordtail hybrid he was trying to invent.

I was no expert. The names were written on labels stuck to the tanks. I also had two foolscap sheets of feeding instructions, written on prison paper by the same neat hand that had cooked a hundred books.

I checked the thermometers and gave them their various

rations of flake food. The colours were nice enough but I could never see them replacing adultery.

Then I called Gordon Gregory's home number in St John's Wood.

I knew he didn't like being disturbed at night but I felt like speaking to somebody. Chatting up fish isn't the same, somehow.

'I've got all the dope on the Abreys,' I said, trying to identify the background noises at his end. I owed a lot to Gordon but I didn't know much about him. Judging from what I could hear he was either entertaining two comedians and a large invited audience of laugh-happy idiots or he was watching television. Somehow I'd thought he'd be too sophisticated for that.

'Very good, James,' he said. He tended to use that superior tone with me, as if he was a much older as well as a much smoother man. In fact we were about the same age. I think it was his subtle way of helping me remember my gratitude.

'What's it all about anyway?' I asked.

'I don't know. What sort of people are they – on the sweaty side I'd imagine, from the address.'

'A cosy little family. I come from the sweat belt myself so maybe I can't see the stains.'

'Boasting again?'

'We'll have to snatch a photograph in the street. I'll get Ray Thoms to go down there in the morning.'

'Then you can let me have a nicely typed report.'

I got myself a can of coke from Rag Trade Reggie's big fridge and switched on Rag Trade Reggie's colour set and sprawled out on Rag Trade Reggie's leather couch, all alone in that big house in Putney, just me and Morecambe and Wise and twelve tanks of high-class minnows.

I rubbed my ankle and tried to remind myself that I was enjoying my new, reformed life.

But there was just a chance that at thirty-three my freedom had come too late.

I didn't seem to have anything to fill it with.

Chapter Two

This job – which later I was to call my Solomon episode, when it became safe to joke – started with a phone call from Gordon Gregory.

'It's an easy little tracing routine,' he said, 'not the kind of work I'm saving you for but I'd say money for old rope, James.'

A couple of hours later I was going into the lift in the big new office block in High Holborn. The fine old legal firm of Venables, Venables, Williams and Gregory, solicitors, occupied the whole of the sixth floor and the rent for that much space wasn't covered by widows' mites.

'Very tasty,' I said, when the glam-gal secretary showed me into Gordon's new office. 'I'm glad I left the dirty raincoat at home.'

'It's not meant to impress people like you,' he said. It could have been a compliment. Not that I would have taken offence. I owed Gordon a lot. Before he pulled me back into the lifeboat I'd been living a hand-to-hand existence.

No, not hand-to-mouth. Of the dribs and drabs I earned in the roughest months not a lot managed to reach my mouth. Even after I stopped boosting the gin trade I still found myself boracic. One hand picked up the few quid I was copping, the other pushed it straight at the restless creditors.

I was only the middle-man. The money and I barely had time to say hullo and good-bye.

Boracic lint – skint. The old rhyming slang. It sounds colourful but the reality was murky grey. I was a young ex-copper, which made me sound bent, a newly-cured gin disposal unit, which made me sound medical, and nobody rushes to employ an inquiry agent (self-appointed) who isn't working as an undercover man behind a Soho bar but is just working there, fullstop.

Temporary barman, temporary van-driver (until they brought out the party balloon and I lost the licence), temporary dance-hall bouncer, apprentice bum, these were just some of the careers I toyed with while my head was spinning and my elbow bending.

Then came Gordon.

I had done one or two little favours for Gordon's father in my Flying Squad days and when that career got kicked into touch the old man had done me one or two little favours in return.

I always did mean to pay it back, of course.

Then the old man retired, or was pushed, and Gordon became the boss. The way these things go I thought that was the end of my odd-job connection with Venables etc.

I also hoped the IOUs might be chucked in a bucket with the rest of Gregory senior's mementoes.

But no. Giving me the elbow wasn't one of the changes Gordon's ego required. He sent for me and said he could use me in a big way. He gave me a cheque for two hundred smackers against future earnings and a letter to guarantee a bank overdraft. He told me about his plans to change the firm's image, which tended to be mouthpiece for bigtime villains, like Rag Trade Reggie.

He confided in me a lot.

I listened and made appropriate faces. He probably opened up to me because I was no threat to his new position. Those offices weren't short of smiling young go-getters any one of whom I would have trusted with my mum's tiara provided his hands were on the table, in handcuffs. I didn't really care why he was keen on me.

I was making a fresh start, sure enough, but something had gone. I just didn't seem to care about anything.

I was joking about the dirty raincoat, of course. Just because I had drifted into the inquiry agent racket didn't mean I had to dress like a sparetime flasher caught in a drizzle . . .

The new decor that Gordon had chosen was clubby, brown

panelling, old sporting prints and fake leather chairs. I supposed the idea was to make it look like anything but a working office. It made me think of old men snoring under *The Times*, which reminded me I was only in my thirties, which would have been good for my morale, if I'd had any.

The last year or so had made me feel older than Tutankhamen, who was everywhere that year, and a lot less shiny.

Arranging himself in the middle of his brass-studded swivel chair Gordon told me about this tracing job. As usual I found it hard to concentrate on what he said for wondering if his legs were doing a razor-job on his trousers.

He was one of the thinnest people I have ever sharpened my eyeballs on.

'This comes to us from a firm we sometimes deal with in Los Angeles,' he drawled, sliding a photostatted sheet across the desk. 'They're vouching for the client.'

A woman called Toni, surname unknown but beginning with A. She had given birth to a baby girl in the maternity ward of St Margaret's Hospital on 6 August, 1969. Husband was dark-haired, possibly a mechanic. They lived then in Plaistow. The client wanted to know if the woman and her husband were still together, if the little girl was still alive, their current whereabouts and as much information about them as discreet inquiries could obtain. Discreet was underlined.

'You don't need me,' I said, 'just phone the hospital secretary, he'll co-operate when he knows it's for a respectable legal firm.'

Gordon raised an eyebrow, not too sure if I was being sarcastic.

'There's more,' he said languidly, 'we're also to supply an up-to-date photograph of the child.'

He made an arch of his long, thin fingers and eyed me as if for the first time. I stared back. Whatever else my shabby past had taught me one thing was never to look too grateful. Gordon's fingers pressed against his nose. He looked like a stick insect asking Jesus for another helping.

'I've got a funny feeling about this one,' he said, in the end. 'S. F. Durstader of Los Angeles handle only the best people, meaning anyone who can afford their rates. Now why would anyone in that income bracket, living in California, be interested in a London woman who had a baby six years ago in a crummy dump of a hospital in the dreary East End?'

'I always knew we were living in darkest Africa,' I said.

Gordon smiled patronizingly. It was a little joke between us, mainly on his side, the difference in our backgrounds. Gordon had been to Eton and one of those Oxford colleges which they pronounced the opposite way from the spelling, just to keep us slobs guessing.

My old man's original country seat was in Dagenham, good old Corn Beef City. The nearest we came to a nob was living two doors down from a convenor of shop stewards at Fords.

When Gordon and I laughed at our little joke we were supposed to be congratulating ourselves on not being snobs. It amused him and, as I say, I owed him a lot.

'Just think about it,' he said, 'how does a rich American even know these people exist? And why pay top money for information and a photograph of a child whose surname they don't know?'

'Perhaps they want a penpal?'

'You can be very droll at times, James. By the way, discreet means they're not to know they are being investigated.'

No melodramatics were required to get at the hospital records. I phoned the secretary of St Margaret's. He told me to confirm my request in writing.

This gave me the pleasure of dictating a letter to Gordon's new secretary, Diane, a fair-haired deb-type with a creamy complexion and extremely good knees. In fact she reminded me a lot of my ex, Jackie, good-looking enough to be a model, posh accent – and she sniffed at my little jokes.

I didn't push it. Jackie's knees were the main reason I married her and four diabolical years had taught me – good knees are not enough!

The next day I phoned the hospital secretary from Dot Wilmington's offices, where I had moved into a little cubby-hole of my own. He told me I must be referring to a Mrs Toni Abrey.

There had been only two girls born on that date and the name of the other mother began with G.

I drove across to Plaistow that morning.

The address I'd been given for the Abreys was easy enough to locate. Juggernaut lorries were driving all over it.

The nearest human outpost in that blasted landscape of roads and building sites for roads was a self-service petrol station artistically disguised as a Moon base on carnival day. A glamorous dolly in hot pants (one of the *great* fashions, for knee-men) was giving out plastic busts of Beethoven or Bobby Moore the footballer, you bought four gallons and you took your choice.

I bought my four gallons and chose Bobby Moore. What would I want with a German player?

Sticking Bobby on the back seat of the Stag I asked the girl about the old houses but she was an out-of-work Australian model.

The Indian manager had only been there four weeks. He suggested that the houses must have been demolished to make way for the six-lane flyover. We might have been talking about the first Roman settlers.

I knew the local authority would have been responsible for rehousing the families evicted to make life easier for forty-ton lorries. At the local council offices a sympathetic girl clerk was generously willing to cut through the bureaucratic pocedures, particularly as my ship was due to leave Tilbury for Sydney that very night and I might never see my long-lost cousins again.

It took her less than an hour to find out that Mr Clifford Abrey and family had been allocated a two-bedroomed flat in Herbert Morrison House, Sutherland Avenue, Bethnal Green.

Which is where we came in . . .

As I climbed into Rag Trade Reggie's simple little four-poster that night I felt an attack of the horrors coming on. For a start I was feeling lonely, possibly because the last time I'd been in a bed that size had been with five other people.

I started to read one of Reggie's Agatha Christie paperbacks.

23

He had all of hers on a shelf in the boudoir, probably for wet nights when the orgy crowd didn't show.

No offence to Agatha but the book didn't hold me. For one thing I'd easily spotted the murderer by page twenty-five and for another I prefer reading about detectives who meet lots of nymphomaniacs.

For another my throat was carrying on something diabolical for a drink.

My ankle was throbbing and two cans of coke were making me burp. I put out the light, then put it on again.

I read another ten pages of Agatha, discovered I'd got the wrong murderer, went to the carsi, kept my eyes on a short leash as I passed the plush bar in the lounge, had another inspection of Reggie's finny friends to make sure they weren't being frozen or steam-cooked or whatever happens to tropicals when the thermostats go on the blink, couldn't think of anyone to phone, and then lay in the dark thinking any old thoughts that came along.

Was this simple little tracing job agitating my conscience, I wondered. What conscience, I asked myself. Wasn't I the geezer who made the resolution about telling lies? Already I'd lied to the Abreys about being a TV researcher and lied to the girl in the council offices about being their long-lost cousin.

And tomorrow I'd be sitting across the road in Ray Thoms's car while he snatched pictures of the kid.

In the old days I'd never lost sleep over *work*, not even when some of the tastiest villains in London had promised faithfully that I'd wake up with my knees nailed to the floor.

That reminded me of Diane's knees. But I still couldn't drop off.

Chapter Three

What happened between Toni Abrey and me was nothing to write home about. Not to her home anyway. At the time I took it as one of the fringe benefits this racket is supposed to be rich in, if you believe all you read . . .

It was the following Monday when it happened. I went into Dot Wilmington's office with a light step and a ready smile.

'A woman called you twice,' said Maureen Pegg, who was Dot Wilmington's office manager. The office was a converted mews house in that pricey area behind Kensington High Street. Dot was a small, ugly woman with more personality than a boatload of disc-jockeys and a lot more brains. I got to know her in my Flying Squad days. She called herself a business efficiency consultant, which is a good cover for her kind of operation.

When I first thought of this racket as my next career she let me use her phone number and even pushed a few small credit-checking jobs my way.

Now that I was getting established she had rented me a converted cupboard as an office. She was a good friend, Dot.

Maureen was the snag.

Maureen was a hefty blonde any man would have been glad to wrestle with, at equal weights. I'd feel sorry for the geezer who tried. What Dot saw in that Nordic bitch I never understood but they lived together as man and wife.

It's usually the older woman who suffers from jealousy in that kind of scene but as far as Dot and men were concerned Maureen was as possessive as an oil sheik with a virgin gusher.

Perhaps she had good reason. Dot might be pushing fifty but you always had the impression she was game for anything . . .

'Who was this woman?' I asked.

'She wouldn't leave her name – she sounded rather common,' said Maureen.

'That's how I like 'em, common and anonymous.'

'I'm sure it is.'

I shrugged and went on up the stairs to my cubby-hole. A desk, a chair, a square yard of worn canvas that carpet beetles had grazed clean, a grey phone and a small window that rattled.

And a wire-basket, for the heavy flow of assignments and cheques.

It still held the same, solitary sheet of paper that had been there the week before, a neatly written letter from Her Majesty's drive-in but don't drive-out on the Isle of Wight.

Down there in Parkhurst Rag Trade Reggie was hopeful of finding foster-parents for his fish but in the meantime I was to pay special attention to tank number six in which, if I was reading correctly, a pair of firemouth cichlids might soon be eating their last lot of babies to make room for a new happy event.

I was to take the young ones in a plastic bag to a tropical fish shop in Shepherd's Bush market. There I was to ask for Mr Mill the owner, and say the fish came from Mr Mancini.

Mr Mill would pay me for the fish and I was to hold the money.

I'd written back to Reggie with the obvious questions. How the hell do I get the baby fish out of the tank? Are the parents friendly to humans or do I insure my fingers?

I skimmed his prison letter back into the empty basket and told myself that I'd better get a gaff of my own. Not a fish gaff – a flat or a room or something. Sharing was no good, especially with parents who cured overcrowding by eating the kids.

The phone rang.

It was Mrs Toni Abrey. She sounded rather shy.

'I've been trying to remember more about the hospital,' she said, 'you did say to ring you, didn't you?'

Her voice was much softer and more feminine on the phone.

'It's funny what comes back to you, innit, things you thought you'd forgotten?'

She sounded almost girlish.

'I'm not sure if it's the kind of thing you're after,' she said.

Neither was I but I was prepared to risk it.

'As it happens I may be over your way tomorrow morning,' I said in business-like fashion. 'Maybe I could drop in, if the lift's working.'

'Well, it's just little things, maybe it won't be much use to your programme.'

'There's only one way to find out. By the way, don't forget what I told you.'

'What's that?'

'Once a day and lightly.'

She laughed, not quite so girlishly.

'You do it your way and I'll do it mine,' she said.

I don't know why I was feeling nervous when I set out next morning for Bethnal Green. She had more to lose than I did. If the worst comes to the worst the man can always do the old up with the trousers and out of the window trick.

From seven floors up?

That's why I was nervous. I'd forgotten my parachute.

Of course I wasn't really nervous. Curious would be more like it. Yeah, curious to see if I could make a come-back.

When she opened the door she smiled with an attractive blush. I was wearing my suede jacket and my give away nothing face. She had been vacuuming. She was wearing a red dress and a light blue apron. Her legs were bare. I watched her nervous movements as she unplugged the machine and shoved it in a cupboard, making the usual apologies women make about the place being in a mess.

Only in her case the place was a mess.

'Don't worry about me,' I said, 'it's Nature who abhors a Hoover.'

She was too flustered to laugh.

'Like a cup of tea?' she asked.

'I'd prefer coffee.'

'How d'you like it?'

'In a cup.'

'Jokes like that I can see why they don't let you get on the screen.'

She went into the kitchen. I was glad she had reminded me I was supposed to be a television researcher. I took off my jacket and sat on the orange settee. The goldfish was still doing energetic laps of its bowl. Perhaps it thought I'd come to the rescue.

'I hope it's not too strong,' she said, handing me a blue cup and saucer, standing over me with the bowl of sugar. My eyes were about level with her knees. She had peculiarly long kneecaps. Her long legs were strong and smooth and white, with just a suggestion of goose-pimples on what I could see of her thighs.

I wasn't staring at them, they just happened to be there, bang in front of my face.

She sat down.

'Have you actually got any information for me?' I asked.

She wasn't as nervous as I'd thought.

'What do I call you?' she asked. 'James sounds silly. Can I call you Jimmy?'

'Only my intimate friends call me Jimmy.'

'That's good.' She smiled. 'Information? What a funny word. It's like that crime programme on the telly, Police Five.'

I took a sip of her rotten coffee and put the cup and saucer on the floor.

'You got any particular crime in mind?' I said, my face straight.

She got up and went to the TV set. She turned the little girl's tinted photograph to the wall.

'How about blindfolding the fish?' I said. She smiled. 'Your husband on the picket line?' I asked. She nodded. 'Strike while the iron is hot,' I murmured, to myself.

There was nothing shy about the way she plonked herself down beside me on the settee. We stared at each other. Her hand reached up and her fingertips traced the outline of my nose.

'Was it broken?' she asked, her voice sounding strained.

'Not when I got it,' I said.

She was staring at my mouth. I leaned forward and licked her lips. They opened. Pressing my mouth softly against hers I slipped my hands through her hair, pulling her face firmly into mine. She was groaning and panting. I thought I could get a sniff of fried bacon.

'Ever since you left Thursday night, I've known I wouldn't be happy till I got you in bed,' she breathed into my ear.

My hands dropped to touch her thighs – and knees. She immediately took hold of them and lifted them to her breasts.

I stood up and pulled her to her feet. I kissed her and then turned her round, my face pressing against her hair. I pulled the sash of her apron and let it fall to the floor. Slowly I pulled at the zip of her dress.

She stepped out of it and turned to face me, sliding her arms round my neck. My thumb and forefinger undid the catch on her bra. She watched me staring at her breasts. Her nipples were large and shiny. Her whole body was strong and smooth and white.

There was something delicate about the way she stood there, hands on the back of my neck, while I got off my clothes.

Then my hands were all over her.

'I love your goose-pimples,' I started to say but she was tired of my brilliant chat.

'I want you now, *please*,' she murmured, savagely.

And she did get me, right there on that awful orange settee. She got more of me than she bargained for.

Without being too clinical, I could do everything *but*, if you follow. I was like an oil drill riding the stormy North Sea but the gusher would not flow.

Not that she noticed. Once, twice – three times – she let out that little cry and crushed me round with her smooth white arms and strong thighs.

'Oh my God it's wonderful,' she moaned.

But I just couldn't let myself go. I don't know why. Maybe it was because every time I lifted my face I could see that damned goldfish peering at me.

We went into the bedroom.

I felt like Superman – but I could not deliver the final zap and wowie.

It didn't help when my head nudged the pillow to one side and I found myself staring at Cliff Abrey's intimate pyjamas. She quickly slung them under the bed and eased her hips under mine and again I was drilling deep into the ocean bed and again she was convulsing.

Why be mealy-mouthed about it? I gave her a terrific seeing-to – six times by her count – but the old rock-python refused to eject his juice.

'Oh my God, I feel like a cat that's had too much cream,' she groaned, lying in my arms, my hands feeling the strength of her warm, white back. We lay there and talked. I kissed her a lot, sometimes on the mouth. We talked some more. She didn't think it more than eccentric that I wanted to kiss and fondle her unusually long kneecaps. We told each other it had never been like this before, ever.

But it hadn't been at all, for me, not yet.

I was near it, though. So I tried again – on Tuesday morning, on Wednesday morning and on Friday morning. Thursday she had to go and see Tricia's teacher. I went into my de luxe cupboard at Dot's place and started planning my business.

Then Gordon rang.

'That report of yours must have been hot stuff,' he said. 'I've just had a cable to say that Mrs Georgina Gunning is arriving at Heathrow tomorrow and can we meet her.'

'Who is Mrs Georgina Gunning?' I asked.

'She's the one who wanted to know about the Abreys. She could only have got our letter with the photographs yesterday. We've to book her a suite at Claridges.'

'Not short of a bob or two then?'

'I told you. Durstader only handle the elite. So do we, if it comes to that.'

'Yeah, the elite of Claridges and Parkhurst. Well, let me know what it was all about.'

'You're coming with me, James. She'll want to ask you about the Abreys.'

'Meeting fairy godmothers off planes isn't exactly what I do best.'

'Why do you say that, fairy godmothers?'

'I dunno. I hope she isn't a fairy godfather.'

'We'll take the firm's car. I'll see you here at half past twelve. We'll be paying you on the usual hourly basis, of course.'

'In that case I'll come early.'

Why did I say that about fairy godmothers? I didn't know. The best I could do in the Agatha line was to assume that whatever was interesting a rich American in the Abreys was bound to do them some good.

It was their lucky week after all. Hers anyway.

On Friday morning Toni did the trick. Simple, really, once she'd thought of it.

'I think you're a bit kinky, James,' she said, pressing her breasts together so that my whole face was in warm darkness.

'Balls,' I muttered from the depths.

'I've never known a man who messed about with my knees, before,' she giggled. 'You're kinky for knees, James. I think you like my knees better than the rest of me.'

I grunted something, as near to embarrassed as you ought to be stretched naked with another man's wife on the other man's bed, in broad daylight. I'd really have preferred the curtains drawn but she said there weren't many peeping toms flying helicopters.

'I don't mind,' she said lovingly, 'I'd do anything for you, James, honest. I've never felt about anyone the way – I just want to make you happy, James. Would it help if you could see my beautiful knees while you're doing it? No, go on, I won't laugh, my darling. Look, you get on top – I saw it in a book of positions – Cliff thought it was disgusting – I put my legs this way – ohhhh, James, let me feel it, my darling, let me feel all of it . . .'

Simple, wasn't it—

I felt like the GPO Tower when the bomb went off.

They say that adultery is only for the wicked? All I know is I was back to beautiful, wonderful *normal*.

I didn't tell her the appointment I was rushing away to keep was with the client who had been reponsible for my first visit. I'd been meaning to tell her but by the time I came out of the spell it was ten past twelve. Explanations would have taken too long.

It didn't seem important, anyway.

'Will I see you Monday, my darling?' she asked, watching me whip into my clothes, stretching out her strong, white body on the crumpled sheets.

'I might be working,' I said. 'You sure you couldn't manage to get over to my place in Putney? It's a bit dangerous, me dropping in here, not being able to phone you first. What if – ' I nodded my head in the direction of the absent Cliff – 'they told him he didn't have to do any more picket duty?'

'Just say you was doing more of your research,' she said, turning over on her stomach, cuddling her face into the pillow. 'I'd have to think up some excuse to be away for the day – it'd be lovely, wouldn't it, just you and me? If only ...' Her cheeks were round and white and smooth. I leaned over and gave the nearest one a kiss. She smiled at me over her shoulder. 'It worked for you, didn't it, James? My knees!' She laughed and wriggled.

'Keep reading the book of positions,' I said. As I stopped at the door she pouted a little kiss at me. I nodded.

Why tell a lie, I didn't think I would be coming back to that warm little bedroom with the balcony over the empty building site.

Didn't I say I was back to normal?

Normally I'm a shit. When they start coming the old love crap that's when I start remembering about work and the chances of being caught. The big slide-out.

I was caught in that love crap trap once in my life.

I'm maybe not brilliant but I don't reckon on making the same mistake twice.

But I would always remember that little bedroom in Herbert's house with gratitude.

When I swung the Stag down the ramp into the basement of the office block in High Holborn I saw the flagpole figure of Gordon Gregory standing by the bonnet of a black Mercedes.

Even in that gloom I could see he wasn't pleased. Behind him was a driver in a uniformed cap. They didn't look as if they'd been sharing a dog-end.

'Sorry, I got caught in a jam,' I said over the car roofs as I locked the Stag.

'Can we get started now? Gordon snapped.

Considering the hold-up had stopped traffic for a mile and a half in Commercial Road I'd made good time getting back from Bethnal Green but seeing Gordon's mood I gave the rest of my apology the day off. It was none of his business anyway. That morning's trip to Herbert Morrison House wouldn't be featuring on my time-sheet.

We got into the Mercedes and set off for London Airport. Gordon's bad temper lasted well into Chiswick. I just settled in my corner and watched the sunshine. Even my ankle felt good.

Gordon kept looking at his watch. Then, sounding relieved, he said:

'He's making good time. I don't think we'll be so terribly late after all.'

'Panicking, were you, squire?' I said cheerfully. 'It's easier than it looks from that high window of yours.'

Neither of us knowing what this woman looked like we arranged for Tannoy messages to call her to the PanAm desk in case we missed her at the disembarkation gate. I saw that Gordon was on edge again.

'It always makes me laugh,' I said.

'Must you be so relentlessly cheery? What makes you laugh?'

'Those TV commercials for flying. Big airliners crammed with unattached beauties and trendy young stallions. The Jet Set? You ever seen so many dumpy, middle-aged men outside of a lunchtime strip show? There's the reality, grumpy computer salesmen, hordes of them all identical, acid on the stomach and corns on the arse.'

'It must be wonderful to have no responsibilities,' he said, almost bitterly. It wasn't the first remark like that he'd made. I was getting the notion his own marriage might not be too kosher.

Then we saw the client.

Nobody could have mistaken Mrs Georgina Gunning for a grumpy dumpy.

She was a tall, elegant lady. She was dressed in black yet the effect was like Technicolor. Her turban hat was black and so was her knee-length silk coat. Big, saucer-shaped sunglasses hid the top half of her face.

From her walk I put her at around forty, which wasn't too far out. Her mouth was set tight and her chin was just beginning to grow a twin. Her hands were heavy with rings.

'Mrs Gunning?' said Gordon.

'Yeah,' she said.

In some ways I'm sharper than others – and that lovely day I was feeling brilliant. Only the one word, *yeah*, and already I was curious about her accent. It sounded American all right but it didn't sound genuine.

Gordon made the introductions. I held out my hand. Perhaps the weight of all those rings was handicapping her. I left my hand in mid-air for a moment, as though I had a fly to catch.

'Can you hustle my baggage through, I really hate airports?' she said. Her voice was quite hoarse. As we started down the stairs she lit a cigarette, flicking a gold lighter before I could play the gent. Her nails were a rich purple but not too well kept.

She seemed very American, very rich and very loud without saying much, if that makes sense. We had to wait twenty long minutes for her cases to come up the belt onto the revolving platform. She didn't wait well. Her black windscreens seemed to stare at us angrily. I tried a light jest or two but she had no sense of humour.

It was not until we were in the Mercedes and sailing through the underpass tunnel that she found it convenient to speak.

'You've seen these Abrey people?'

'James has – he did the report,' said Gordon, who had insisted on taking the fold-down seat and was facing us both.

'Pretty slummy was it?' she drawled at me.

'Depends what you're used to,' I said airily, looking out of the window. I don't like tough women, I decided.

Then she surprised all present.

'I'm used to it all right, cock,' she snapped.

34

There wasn't the slightest trace of America in her voice. She was a cockney!

'What's the husband like?' she asked, back in American.

'Fairly nondescript,' I said.

'With black hair? Looks a bit like Hitler?'

Then I got it. The other baby girl, born on 6 August, six years ago in St Margaret's, whose parents' surname began with G.

'You were in the same maternity ward,' I said.

She nodded.

Chapter Four

Georgina Gunning was tighter with words than a Paris waiter with change but during the car ride we got a little more out of her, strictly at her own speed. She was a Londoner and had emigrated to America with her husband, who was something in the music business.

Her reluctance to chat was making Gordon very tense. He was practically twitching in the fold-down seat.

Maybe it was the close-up view of so much leg that was agitating him.

I sneaked the odd sideways glance myself. The way women's fashions have gone it wasn't often you saw a yard or two of nyloned thigh and well-rounded fetlock.

Her knees were on the broad side but not fat. Nothing, however, to excite a man in my state of mind.

As we booked her into Claridges and then went up in the lift I could see she was no stranger to the high life. Naturally I was curious. That's a big jump, the East End to Claridges, via Los Angeles.

From the way she dealt with the porter I could see that the words please and thanks had been lost somewhere along the line.

Gordon started to say something about it being her first night in London and how he'd be delighted to take her out to dinner.

'Just tell me when you can fix up for me to see these people, the Abreys,' she snapped.

Gordon looked at me. I took my time about lowering myself into one of Mr Claridge's easy chairs and lighting a cigarette. That morning's little gallop was helping me recapture some of my old winning ways.

'So – when do I get to see them?' she demanded.

'It's easy enough,' I said, 'you ring a little bell and they open the door. He's the one with the bad breath.'

Her big round glasses swivelled on to me. I was supposed to quiver like a bale of hay facing a flame-thrower. When she saw the cool way I blew smoke at the ceiling, giving my chest a scratch at the time, she turned her back and took off the overcoat. She was wearing a plain brown dress, the seat crumpled from the flight.

She raised her arms to take off the turban hat. Then she spoke. Her accent had settled somewhere out there where the big waves roll.

'It's important that I see them as quickly as possible, without them seeing me,' she said deliberately. 'How do I do it?'

'You could wear a false beard,' I suggested.

She almost clenched her fists. Then she pulled off the hat. Her red hair was in a tightly-pinned chignon. She turned towards us, throwing the hat onto the chintzy sofa.

'Perhaps you can give me some idea of what your interest in the Abreys is,' Gordon said, humbly.

I began to get the idea he was just a little bit scared of her.

She took off the shades and blinked. I'm always suspicious of people who hide behind dark glass. Opticians will tell you our sun is never bright enough to damage healthy eyes. Maybe it's brighter in California but that's five thousand miles away. Besides, even Claridges don't provide a room with a glare.

'I'm sorry,' she said, 'but I have to see them for myself before I can tell you anything. That's the way it is. Do you have any suggestions or shall I make my own arrangements?'

'Oh no, we'll be only too happy to carry out our instructions and help you in every possible way,' said Gordon, creeping bastard.

I could see by then what she had been hiding. Puffy eyes. Either she was a lush or she'd spent the whole flight from Los Angeles watching a weepy movie.

And as anybody could tell she was no sob-sister I took it we had one of those problem housewife drinkers on our hands.

'We can wait outside the block tomorrow morning,' I said

after Gordon had given me an urgent look. 'I'll pick you up here about ten.'

Then I left Gordon to it, glad I was only the doorstep snooper with the dodgy table manners, the man nobody asked to dinner.

As it turned out I was both right and wrong about Mrs Gunning. She *had* been crying a lot and she *did* know the quick way to drain a gin bottle . . .

It was a quarter to eleven on Saturday morning. Her eyes were hidden behind the big dark bins and I couldn't see if a night's kip had improved them.

We were sitting in the Stag watching the front entrance of Herbert Morrison House, the car parked thirty yards up on the other side of Sutherland Avenue, both of us wearing shades, enough tinted glass between us for a pop star's Rolls-Royce.

I stared through the various panes separating me from the street. After a diabolical spring, which followed one of those mild winters that gets old twits saying *we'll pay for it later*, summer had come in earnest.

The East End pavements were busy with Saturday morning people, unshaven men in cardigans, men in slippers reading newspapers, smart young mums with prams and headscarves protecting curlers for Saturday night out, big boys with long hair and Arsenal scarves dangling from their belts, two teenage coppers in shirt sleeves, an old geezer with a crippled spine, walking with his face and chest parallel to the ground.

'Why don't they let the child out to play?' Mrs Gunning said irritably. 'You don't get so much damn sunshine over here you can afford to waste it.'

She said this with her American accent. Sometimes she was all-American – I reely hate errpoarts? – sometimes true East End and more often a mixture. It seemed to have something to do with her moods.

As far as my own were concerned I was becoming more patriotic every time she opened her lipsticked mouth.

'This car's cramping me,' she said, giving my new upholstery a pounding with her trousered backside.

'Everything's smaller in England,' I murmured.

'Especially people's minds.'

Now that we were relaxed enough to be merely hostile I asked her where Gordon had taken her for dinner. What I really wanted to know was why she was interested in the Abreys.

'Some Mayfair place,' she sneered.

'That bad, was it?'

'I wasn't in the mood for gallantry.'

'That's only his professional manner.'

'What's he like off-duty?'

'I dunno, he never takes me to dinner in Mayfair.'

She snorted. During all this her eyes never once left the front entrance of Herbert's house. Gradually I started pumping her.

Her husband Alan had been a pop musician who didn't quite make the big money. When his group folded he tried his hand at producing records. Two of these had made the charts and he had then been offered a job by an independent label in Los Angeles. Out there he had been responsible for four or five global smasheroos.

She seemed surprised that I'd never heard of any of them.

'You must be a real dead body,' she said. 'They've sold millions but you've never heard of them?'

'I sleep a lot. Anyway, you've done quite well over there?'

'According to the trades Alan is dragging down quarter a million dollars a year.'

'The trades?'

'The music trade papers. I read them to keep up with our lives.'

Her voice had gone quiet and bitter. I said nothing. She bit her lips.

'How many kids they expect to pack into that stinking apology for a playground?' she said. 'One thing I'd forgotten, how many blacks you have in London.'

'Bother you, do they?'

'Give my Alan his due, he wasn't going to sit on his ass and let his kids grow up in a dump like this. Aren't these bloody people ever going to appear? I'll bet he's the kind of slob who stays in bed all weekend.'

'As a matter of fact he turned down a trip to Paris with his mates rather than deprive the kid of a day in the park. They should be showing soon. How many kids do you have?'

The big shades stayed beamed on Herbert's house.

'Just the one?' I said.

'I had three miscarriages before – Helen. The doctors say I can't have any more. I'm pushing forty you know. Don't say it, I look older.'

'Who's looking after your little – '

Simultaneously we saw them, Cliff and Toni Abrey. Behind them came two little girls, holding hands.

Mrs Gunning took in a sharp breath and leaned forward, fingers touching her lips.

'Oh God,' she said, almost moaning, 'that awful dress, don't they even know how to – oh God!'

For a moment I was puzzled. How did she know which of the girls was Patricia Abrey? Then I remembered the photographs. I was reading too much Agatha.

'They're going the other way,' she said, starting to open the door on her side. 'We'll lose them!' Just for a moment she was almost hysterical.

'He's going to the car park,' I said calmly. 'See the holdall? That's the picnic. The other kid belongs to a neighbour. You seen enough?'

'No, follow them!' she yelped, sounding like a different woman altogether.

As I'd always been careful to park the Stag a couple of streets away from the block I was pretty sure Toni did not know what kind of car I drove – and in any case I still had the vague idea that Mrs Gunning was bringing the Abreys a nice big surprise. Maybe she wanted to share some of her husband's greenbacks with the friendly woman she remembered from the next maternity bed. No maybes about one thing, however, at five guineas an hour I didn't have anything better to do on a Saturday anyway.

It was an easy tailing job. There was no mistaking Cliff Abrey's car, a two-door Ford hand-painted in shiny black. He was no Fittipaldi, the hardest part was keeping far enough back not to bang him up the khyber. At that speed he should have been done for illegal parking.

'Christ, those damn lights!' Mrs Gunning wailed when we were caught by two reds in succession along Barking Road.

'No problem,' I said, 'I know where he's going even if we do lose him.'

'Yeah? How come you know so much about them? You didn't bug their flat or anything, did you?'

'I didn't have to,' I said but she was not really interested.

When we got to Valentine's Park in Ilford cars were already standing bumper to bumper along the asphalt road that leads towards the bandstand. Men and boys were streaming towards the big marquee of the cricket ground.

I saw where Cliff had parked the little Ford and then we lost sight of them for a few minutes while I found space for the Stag.

We walked into the park. From behind the tent came the rippling noise of cricket enthusiasts waking up to clap a good stroke.

I saw the Abreys, Cliff leading the little party towards the trees on a slope that led down to the boating lake. Toni was wearing black slacks and a white cardigan.

I took off my suede jacket in case she recognized it. We were about seventy yards away, on the other side of the lake, but I wasn't taking any chances.

We watched them spread out on the grassy slope.

'This is as near as I go,' I said, flopping down.

'You wait here and I'll have a walk round the pond.'

'Take the short cut,' I said, quietly, to her back.

I'd known this park as a boy and nothing much seemed to have changed, except for transistors and myself. So strong were the memories I had to remind myself I was not little Jim-Jim with his jar for tiddlers but James Hazell, inquiry agent, engaged on serious grown-up business, if anybody would tell me what the business was.

The Abreys were on the highest part of the bank, their blanket spread out under a big oak. Toni lay flat out with an open book shielding her face.

I could see Mrs Gunning, the mystery woman from Los Angeles, circling the pond, looking alone and conspicuous.

Was it actually a quarter of a century ago I'd last looked over this stretch of water? The same shirt-sleeved men in braces were rowing anxious wives and children who wouldn't sit still in the hired boats.

The same little boys crouched knees to chin and toes to water, pushing out their toy yachts, flailing at the water with nets which never seemed to catch anything.

I'd had lots of friends then.

I saw the two little girls throwing a tennis ball, under-arm, as girls do. Tricia's friend missed her catch and the ball bounced down the slope and across the path into the water.

Both girls scampered down the bank. I saw Cliff sitting up. The girls were running so fast it looked as if they couldn't stop. Cliff shouted something, rising on one knee.

Was he genuinely wrapped up in that little girl – or was she just something to hold on to, something to fill the emptiness?

The girls stopped dead at the water's edge. I saw Toni raising her head to see what the fuss was about.

Poor Toni. Married to a guy who bored her when he wasn't irritating her. I guessed what kind of book she would be reading, a romance with strong men who had aquiline features and crinkly smiles and saw the hidden beauty of the ugly duckling with the specs and the terrible shyness.

'If it wasn't for Tricia . . .' she'd said, over and over again.

Three teenagers in a rowing boat had pulled the floating ball towards them with an oar and were teasing the girls, threatening to keep it. Mrs Gunning was coming round the far end of the lake.

Cliff got to his feet and started down the slope. The boys threw the ball towards the bank and rowed away, laughing so raucously I could hear them on this side.

Cliff picked up the ball and bounced it dry. Then he took the girls off in the direction of the cafeteria.

They passed a bench on which sat Mrs Gunning, the lady in the big dark glasses.

Her head swivelled to follow them but she stayed on the bench.

Lucky Jim? If Jackie and I had kids, would we have stuck it out together?

A few moments later the girls came running back with ice-cream cones, heading along the side of the pond. Far behind came Cliff, the ice-cream in each hand making him walk like a man on a rope across Niagara. As Toni had said, he should have been the mother.

Something happened as the girls approached the seat. Maybe it was the heat or the reflection of the water but I had a strange sensation I was seeing these small figures moving in slow motion, like a dream.

Tricia's friend must have dropped her ice-cream. Mrs Gunning got to her feet and walked towards them. When she was a couple of yards away she must have said something. Both girls turned their heads to look at her.

Then they were standing together, the tall woman in the dark glasses and the two girls in their summer frocks. I couldn't be sure but I thought Mrs Gunning put her arm round Tricia's shoulders.

Then she was giving them something from her white handbag. The girls ran back towards the cafeteria. Cliff shouted and they veered towards him, scampering over the grass. They pointed.

Cliff will get a surprise when she takes off the shades and gives him the big hello, I thought.

But she didn't.

As soon as she saw the kids talking to Cliff Mrs Gunning turned away and started walking round the lake.

The girls ran off. Cliff stood there, indecisively as always, an ice-cream in each hand. From here I could tell he was frowning moronically.

Then the girls came back with fresh cones and the three of them walked up the bank towards Toni, Cliff still staring after Mrs Gunning.

I got up and ambled towards the park entrance, wiping my

forehead with my handkerchief. My ankle was creaking.

Mrs Gunning didn't speak until we got into the ovenheat of the Stag. Her mouth was tight, just a suggestion of a tremble about her lips.

'It is her,' she said, staring straight ahead.

I waited but she hadn't been speaking to me.

We drove away from the park. I found we couldn't turn right for Central London at the Romford Road junction.

'We'll go down Ilford Lane and pick up the Barking Road,' I said. It didn't matter a damn to her. She stared ahead, hands clasped across her stomach, fingers tightly locked, knuckles showing white against her suntan. Factory buildings passed on either side of us.

'I need a drink,' she said at last.

'We'll be back at the hotel in half an hour.'

'No, now.'

'I haven't any in the car, sorry.'

'Stop at the first bar.'

'This is East Ham, not a lot of elegant cocktail lounges to choose from.'

'I know this is East bloody Ham,' she snapped, 'I know this road better than I know my . . .'

Her voice faded away.

We came to a small corner pub, one of the old kind the tartening-up brigade had not yet vandalized, frontal decor by soot and rain and the lifted hindlegs of whole generations of roving mongrels, brown tiles and frosted glass windows with hand-coloured posters advertising gala nights with three-piece groups.

We parked in the side street. The tension was coming off her in waves.

Inside the colour scheme was wartime brown and not the Hitler war either. The arrival of a woman in blue trousers, white silk scarf and dark glasses made heads turn. It was the kind of pub that serves as a communal living-room for the whole street. Any new face would have been conspicuous.

We skirted a bunch of men at the bar and found a wet table.

'Large gin on the rocks,' she said, in loud American.

I moved into the rows of men defending the bar against all-

44

comers. Most of them were craning their necks to watch a TV set perched on a side wall.

The runners were under orders for the one-thirty at Cheltenham. Off! Men began shouting, egging on their selections, waving fists, giving out hysterical shouts ... 'go on my son ... pull away, pull away ... git the whip aht! ... push 'im me little beautee ...'

Two men on stools clenched imaginary reins and slapped the seats of their trousers.

I inched closer to the bar, holding a pound note above two men drinking ear to ear. The race finished to boos and a few isolated cheers. The barmaid, a gay old thing with false eyelashes and a bra that couldn't be burned in case she tripped over them, homed towards my pound.

'Usual luv,' bawled a ruddy-faced man with a handkerchief on his head, knotted at each corner.

'Fred! Make 'at annuvver free an' two pintsa legs, myte,' roared one of his mates.

'Excuse me, squire,' I said.

'Sure me old cocker.'

He moved at least an inch.

'Large gin and a grapefruit juice, love,' I said.

Christ knows what merriment a request for ice would have caused.

Moving back from the bar with the glasses and a bottle of tonic I had to edge through a wave of newcomers, all of them in their undervests, their heads white with plaster-dust, one even stripped to the waist.

I put the drinks on the unsteady formica. Beer tried to drip onto the knees of my pale blue cords.

She said something which I couldn't catch above the din. She picked up the gin and drained half of it down in one big tilt. Trying to keep my shirt dry I leaned forward.

Her face was expressionless, at least the half I could see.

'She is mine,' she said, her voice raised enough to carry over Johnny Cash on the jukebox and the deafening smalltalk. I was glad of the noise. In a quieter place her voice would have been a breach of the peace.

'I didn't believe it but it's true,' she said, 'when I saw her – I *knew*! Oh God, what am I going to do?'

I frowned, sensing many eyes on my back.

'You think I wouldn't know?' she demanded, her voice getting shriller. 'My own flesh and blood?'

I got her out of the Sly Fox. Our departure was followed by witty remarks and jolly laughter from the ghostly powdered plasterers and their sophisticated friends.

Sitting in the car, in the side street, she began to talk. I just sat and listened and looked at the smart set who had brought their pints out onto the pavement. When she finished I could only shake my head.

But when I looked at her I could see she was in deadly earnest.

She said she had to see Gordon Gregory *immediately*. I didn't bother to explain that his weekends were what he called 'sacrosanct'. I drove towards the City until I saw a phone box.

I was out of the car faster than a rat up a rafter.

She could be barmy or she could have been seeing too many old Lana Turner movies on TV. Either way Gordon could have her.

Chapter Five

A woman answered the phone.

'Is Gordon in?' I said.

'Who's calling?' said the snooty voice.

'My name's Hazell, I'd like to speak to Mr Gregory,' I said politely, not sure if she was a servant or a visiting duchess.

'Is it to do with the office?' Before I could reply she added smartly, 'He can't speak to you.'

'Is that Mrs Gregory?' said my honeyed tones.

'Yes but he never takes business calls at the weekend,' she snapped. 'Please ring him on Monday at the office.'

'I'm afraid this is –'

'Are you deaf?'

She rang off!

Gordon had often told me how much he looked forward to getting home to St John's Wood and shutting the door on the sordid villainy of this town.

That was just too bad. What was I supposed to say to this millionaire hysteric – your expensive London lawyer can't come out to play because his wife won't let him?

Half an hour later I was pulling the Stag into the kerb in front of the Gregory residence in St John's Wood. It was a square, neo-Georgian house, red brick and white woodwork, standing well back from the road.

It was a leafy street, no litter in the gutters, no dirty milk bottles on the front steps, no rusting cars, no juggernaut lorries, no ice-cream speakers blaring out *Greensleeves*, no hawkers, no canvassers, no dogs, no kids.

It was hard to believe we were still in the same town as the pub with the half-stripped plasterers. In most of the houses the upstairs windows were closed. There was hardly a car in sight.

This was the class that could lash out sixty or seventy grand on a mansion to escape from the squalor of the big city and *then* dig up a few more thousand for a country cottage so that they could escape from the mansion.

As streets go it made cemeteries seem neighbourly.

I opened the wrought-iron gate and we walked down a flagstone path. On either side stretched free-range billiard baize. The front door was mainly glass. I pressed a neo-Georgian buzzer.

Somewhere behind us, far beyond the lawn sprinklers, London Town's millions swarmed and teemed under a dusty haze but all we could hear were bees buzzing over the catmint.

A beautiful, half-naked girl opened the door. She had black hair, deep brown eyes and the kind of smile that would corrupt an archbishop.

The top half of her white bikini was missing and the bottom half wasn't hiding anything but essentials. Her exquisitely smooth shoulders and boyishly-firm breasts glistened with drops of water.

Unfortunately she was about eight years old.

'We want to see your daddy,' I said.

'The parents and their friends are having drinks in the garden,' she said grandly.

'I'm a friend of your daddy.'

'You had better follow me then.'

We went through the style of house I expected – too much good taste for old slippers and not quite big enough for Buckingham Palace – and stopped at some french windows.

The Gregorys had people in, as they would class it, three or four young couples and an assortment of little Tarquins and Fionas. The lawn stretched down to a weeping willow. Brown lattice-work surrounded the whole garden, as if that class of neighbour would do anything so vulgar as peep over a hedge.

For the kids there was a bright blue paddling pool in which you could have dipped sheep, a set of swings, a slide, and a fleet of pedal cars and tricycles. The adults were clustered decoratively on deck-chairs and sun-beds beside a stone patio on which was a random selection of wrought-iron garden furniture, all in white.

I couldn't see a barbecue.

Gordon's face went red.

The other faces turned in our direction. Gordon stood up. He was wearing a crisp white shirt, a neckerchief, cavalry twill trousers and fawn suedes.

I saw him having a torrid little exchange with a slim black-haired woman in a white blouse and blue yachting trousers.

He must have won that round on points.

'Oh, it's you,' he was saying as he came towards us across the patio, his face flustered but trying hard to look imperturbable. 'We were expecting – Mrs Gunning, would you like to come out for a drink?'

'Sorry about breaking in like this,' I said, not too apologetically, 'I think we should – '

'I could use a cool one,' said Mrs Gunning, in pure American.

Most of the young fathers politely raised well-tailored buttocks an inch or two as we were introduced. Gordon's wife forced herself to nod. Mrs Gunning asked for a gin. I said anything in the soft line would do me.

Gordon went into the house. For a few interesting moments we were left with Mrs Gregory and her socially acceptable friends. She stared at Mrs Gunning and said nothing of a hostess nature. Mrs Gunning more or less ignored all present, staring, as far as I could tell behind the glasses, down the garden where the future supertax dodgers were romping decorously.

Mrs Gregory was the type they call fine-boned. From the icy way she surveyed Mrs Gunning I began to get the notion that she was going to have words with Gordon after we left.

Now she could see the client she was preparing, as wives do, to demand why Gordon had subtly led her to believe that his dreary business dinner was with a combination of Winnie the Witch and Doris Karloff.

My marriage didn't last long but educationally it was a crash-course.

One of the matronly young wives spoke to me, with the kind of South Kensington gurgle that sickens whole busloads.

'Are you Mr Hazell the private detective who works for Gordon?' she asked, with some amusement.

That got everybody's attention.

'Inquiry agent is the trade term,' I said politely.

'But you do have to work among all those awful gangsters and people?' she brayed gaily. 'How absolutely fascinating! You must be really *awfully* tough.'

Gordon was coming back across the patio with our drinks on a small tray. I looked at him as I spoke.

'Yeah well, it's okay when they aint puttin' the boot in an' freatenin' to remove your kneecaps wiv a shotgun an' that,' I said.

Silly, really, but it never occurred to me that he used me as conversational material.

Gordon showed a lot of courage. He didn't suggest that the three of us go inside for at least four minutes, during which I was asked a few equally choice questions. I cooled the act down to brutal grunts.

'I hope you won't be stuck in there all afternoon,' Gordon's fine-boned wife said to our retreating backs. The others chattered madly, possibly about my lack of razor scars.

Gordon led us into his study. Instead of sporting prints the walls were hung with family portraits but otherwise it was like his office. Perhaps he had the soul of a much older man.

He didn't say anything about my Kray Bros act.

I positioned myself carefully in an easy chair under the window. There wasn't a lot of sun coming through the venetian blinds but what there was I was going to need to shield my face. Mrs Gunning and Gordon sat facing each other. She did not take off the dark glasses. Then she started speaking in a low voice. I watched Gordon's face.

'About five weeks ago we drove up to San Francisco for the weekend,' she said. 'One of Alan's groups was on at the Cow Palace and we thought it would be a nice trip for Helen.

'On the way back we had an accident. I was tired, I was too close to the car in front, when it stopped I couldn't brake quick enough. Anyway we hit it. Helen wasn't wearing a safety belt, she was between us on the front seat.

'She was thrown through the windscreen. She had terrible cuts, all over her face and neck.

'When they got her to the hospital she needed a massive blood transfusion. Naturally Alan and I said we wanted them to use our blood so they took samples from both of us.

'One of the things the doctor said – well, he asked if Helen was adopted. We were in a pretty emotional state as you can imagine, Alan shouted at the doctor to forget his bloody paperwork – the doctor said it wasn't that, anyway there must have been a mistake with our blood samples and as there wasn't time to check again they used their own blood bank. You can imagine we weren't paying much attention to things like that – as long as Helen was being taken care of.'

She faltered. Gordon asked her if she would like another drink. She shook her head. He didn't ask me. I lit a cigarette and wondered how often she'd told this story. It sounded well-practised.

'We asked the doctor what he'd meant about Helen being adopted but he said in the rush the blood samples must have got mixed up in the lab.

'Anyway, it stuck in my mind and a couple of weeks later I phoned him. So he said Alan and I should stop by and have our blood groups tested again.

'So we did. There hadn't been any mistake. I don't know if you're familiar with blood groups but simply the situation was that Helen's group was A1. Alan's was O and mine was B.'

'They're the common groups, aren't they?' said Gordon.

'Yes, they are. But the fact is that parents who are O and B cannot produce a child with A1 blood.

'There was just no way Helen could have been born to Alan and myself. He could be her father or I could be her mother – but only one of us could be her parent.'

Gordon looked at me and I nodded slowly. He was beginning to understand why I'd crashed in so rudely on the drinkies scene.

'You don't have to tell me the obvious answer,' she went on, looking down at the Chinese carpet. 'It was what the doctor thought and it was what Alan thought. I'd had the baby – so who was the real father?'

The dark glasses swivelled slightly to see what effect all this was having on me. I hoped I was only a silhouette against sunshine. Gordon fidgeted uneasily. He was thinking up smooth ways of telling her to see a good doctor specializing in woman's troubles. Or so I assumed at the time.

'Well, I can tell you, I was not having it off with any other man,' she said, her voice flat and emphatic. 'I've been married to Alan for seven years and I've been one hundred per cent faithful. You have to take my word on that – I know there's no way I could prove it in a court of law. But it's the truth, I swear it.'

'Oh,' said Gordon. 'So you think – '

'I don't think, Mr Gregory, I know. Ask Mr Hazell, he'll tell you, he's seen the Abrey child. Look!'

She took off the glasses. With a dramatic movement of her free hand she tore at her chignon. If it had been long enough she would have shoved her red hair in our faces.

Gordon looked at me.

'It is the same colour, more or less,' I said.

'Of course it is,' Mrs Gunning snapped. 'She's my baby. She's got Alan's eyes and my hair and anybody who doesn't see us together and admit it is blind or lying. I know it takes a bit of swallowing but that's how it is. Don't you understand? We left that hospital with the wrong babies!'

'But how – is that possible?' Gordon said, frowning.

'It has to be possible. It happened.'

'But surely – I mean, you would have known?'

'You don't think I've asked myself that a thousand times?' Her voice was under control again. 'You go into the delivery room,' she said. 'If you're having a bad labour they give you gas. I was five and a half hours in labour. Then they showed me this wet little thing wrapped in a blanket and told me I'd had a perfectly healthy baby girl. I was so doped up they could have shown me any baby from a million – but let's assume they showed me my own baby, right?

'Now the next time I saw her was back in the ward that night. They brought in my baby, all dry and shiny and wrapped up. She had her name on sticky tape round her wrist.

'It was a baby girl and it had Gunning on the sticky tape and

I'd only seen a wet little thing, remember? When I was exhausted and full of gas?

'So they must have been switched before I saw her for the second time. After that she never left me – I mean, Helen is the baby I took home from St Margaret's.

'And I'll tell you something else. Everybody always remarked on it, Helen doesn't take after you or Alan, they said. Her hair is black, I mean really *jet black*? My God, I know now why it was so black. This morning, in the park? That man Abrey – his hair is black, too damn right it is!'

The door of Gordon's study banged open. It was the tot-sized Delilah with the scandalous bikini arrangement. I gave her a jolly uncle smile.

'Mummy is angry and says are you going to be rude to your guests much longer,' she announced imperiously. Given ten years I'd have switched her all right.

'Excuse me a minute,' Gordon said, going out after his precocious beauty.

Mrs Gunning and I sat there, occasionally catching each other's eye but finding nothing to say. I was thinking this must be the easiest forty guineas I'd ever picked up. I wondered if it would be going it a bit strong to ask for Saturday time and a half.

When Gordon came back he seemed more relaxed. He shut the door and stood beside the empty fireplace.

'I see,' he said wisely. 'Supposing all this is exactly the way you say it is, Mrs Gunning, what – well, I'll put it bluntly, what do you plan to do about it?'

'What do I plan to do about it? For God's sake! What do you think? I should shrug and forget the whole thing?'

'Well, what else – '

'Leave my little girl to be brought up in that dump – by those two? I want my child, Mr Gregory, my own flesh and blood child. Until I saw her this morning I didn't really know what I wanted, I was still in a kind of dream – but I know now.'

I thought it was time I gave Gordon a little help.

'You can hardly just walk in and say, sorry folks, we got the wrong babies and I want mine back,' I said, not making it sound too cheerful.

She glared at me. Gordon glared at me. I shrugged. Gordon did a lot of thinking. I could tell that by the intellectual way his lips waltzed up and down with each other.

'Wouldn't it be best – ' he hesitated, looking down at her with just the right amount of sympathy, 'I mean, on the face of it, wouldn't it be best for all concerned to leave the situation the way it is?'

She shook her head slowly.

'I couldn't do it,' she said quietly. 'I even told myself that's what I ought to do – but I'd be thinking of her, every single waking moment, my own flesh and blood, wondering what's she doing, is she happy, are they bringing her up right, stuck in that dump? No, I couldn't do it. Maybe I'd like to, maybe I wish to God that goddam accident had never – but it's no use, Mr Gregory, I've made up my mind. I want my child and I don't care what it costs or who it hurts.'

I lit a cigarette and blew smoke into the slats of the venetian blinds. I stood up and eased a couple of slats apart just enough to see the little Jonathans and Melissas sliding and swinging in the sunshine. The grown-up versions were sharing an amusing jest. I had always thought they only laughed like that for the benefit of hunt ball photographers. Even from there Gordon's wife looked like the highly-strung type.

'Well, Mrs Gunning,' said Gordon finally, 'this isn't the kind of case we specialize in – '

Smooth but firm, I thought, I like it. I wondered how much he'd charge her for the privilege of being told to go somewhere else. Like a funny farm.

' – but what I'd like you to do is let me think about it until Monday, I'll do some reading into the various precedents – although frankly I can't remember reading of a similar case. Suppose we say my office at ten on Monday?'

'Earlier the better for me,' she said.

'One thing – don't talk about this to anyone. Cases involving babies, custody disputes – they're very big news. If we have a case on our hands my aim would be to solve it with the minimum of public attention.'

'Fat chance,' I snorted.

They both looked at me. I think I was still a bit shirty at being used as a tame thug for witty dinner-table chat.

'Can't you see the headlines?' I said. 'Tug of love baby? Is blood thicker than love? American pop moguls tear London child from mother's bosom? You'd be lucky to come out of it only half as popular as Countess Dracula.'

'I told you already,' she said firmly, without anger, no trace of hysteria, 'I want my baby and I don't care what price has to be paid. I've thought of all the angles. You can't scare me off.'

I looked at Gordon but whatever he was thinking it didn't show.

He couldn't be taking all this seriously, could he? No, course not. He'd put on a few meetings, dig up a few legal items and then bung in a nice bill for doing nothing.

I had a job suppressing a hearty smile. Just supposing this woman's cot and bull yarn got out, no need to guess who would top Cliff Abrey's list of people to be strangled in the morning.

And what could I be saying to calm him down?

– Sorry, me old cocker, I know I said I was from the telly an' that actually I was sussing out a snatch operation on little Tricia, the light of your life. That's right, she comes with us. Oh yeah, and by the way, mate, I might as well own up, I've been charvering your missus . . .

If you've taken the Linguaphone course in cockney you'll know what charvering means. And carsi. Only Mrs Gunning called it the john.

Gordon and I were alone for the first time.

'Sorry about this,' I said as we stood in the hall, 'she insisted on seeing you. Some yarn, eh?'

'Be careful what you say to her,' he said.

'Don't worry, squire, those rich nuts are dangerous.'

'That's not the way we talk about clients,' he said pompously. Before I had a chance to dig him in the ribs she reappeared from the carsi.

55

I drove her back to Claridges and dropped her at the front entrance. When the guy with the gold braid round his black topper opened the door for her we said good-bye but hardly looked at each other. She knew what I thought.

It didn't matter. We wouldn't be meeting again.

That's what I thought.

Chapter Six

A funny thing happened that Sunday morning as I was lying in the four-poster thinking how much I detested Sunday mornings.

Who should come hammering at the front door of Reggie's plush Putney residence but the law, three of them, hard-faced CID types breathing heavily at the prospect of feeling somebody's collar.

And who should be in charge of the team but that big red-faced Aberdonian, Choc Minty? I knew the bastard well from the old days . . .

Before I could get into Reggie's shot-silk dressing-gown the ringing had changed to a steady pounding.

'Keep your hair on,' I shouted as I went down the stairs. The hammering grew louder. I was a couple of weeks behind with the milk money but this was ridiculous.

Preparing to give the dairyman a right volley I slipped the various chains and bolts Reggie felt necessary with his kind of friends.

'Hullo, Hazell,' snapped the hard Scotch voice. I knew then it wasn't the Express Dairy's bad debt squad. My eyes winced blearily at all the free-range sunshine. 'We'd like a word.'

Chocolate Minty! He got the nickname from some caper involving a hi-jacked lorryload of fruit and nut bars. I gathered we were not to have a jolly re-union.

There's nothing bothers a serving copper more than an ex-cop who didn't wait for the pension – or was pushed. And Choc Minty had never fancied me, even when we were detective-constables together.

To put it simply he thought I was bent.

The next half hour was heavy.

They had come to do me for organizing Reggie Mancini's escape from Parkhurst!

It was those letters about the fish. Reggie had replied to my urgent plea for instructions, repeating all that stuff about contacting a fish shop in Shepherd's Bush market.

And when the screw who censors the letters read the details of how to net baby fire-mouths in tank number six he had rapidly concluded this was code for a mass break-out!

I knew better than to laugh in Minty's face.

While his two aides turned the house over for plans of the prison, rope ladders, machine-guns and recipes for hollow cakes I showed Minty tank number six and the baby fire-mouths and told him how the parents would soon start eating them, out of parental love for the next lot.

I showed him Reggie's aquarist's manuals but he didn't laugh at my little crack about fishy books being Reggie's speciality.

I explained why I was living there and as a clincher told him to ring Gordon Gregory's home number.

Minty's red face registered as much emotion as a weighing machine listening to a hard luck story.

He told one of the detective constables to keep me out of the room while he phoned. I presumed he was calling Gordon. I stood on the landing with the silent detective constable and tried not to wriggle my bare toes.

Then the door opened.

'All right, come in here,' Minty said in thick Aberdonian. My bare feet slid across the carpet of the big lounge. Minty stood by the window and eyed me with all the friendliness of an impatient axe.

It isn't easy to put up a confident front for a professional hard man like Minty when you're wearing nothing but a poncy dressing-gown.

I sat on the big leather couch and covered my bare legs. I felt like a Girl Guide caught with her knicks down.

'You lads want to wait in the car?' Minty said, ignoring my provocative ankles.

I hear the front door bang. Suddenly it was very quiet.

'I wondered when you'd turn up again,' Minty said.

'Missing me, were you?'

We stared at each other.

'Your host run to whisky?' he said. 'Never too early, is it?'

I nodded in the general direction of Reggie's bar, a white leather and black chrome job that could have handled a Glasgow football fans' cocktail party with room to spare.

Minty walked over and got himself a glass of neat malt deep enough for drowning pups.

'Yourself?'

'I've given it up.'

He stood in front of the empty fireplace, examining me and the whisky in turns.

'I thought you went a bundle on this stuff,' he said.

'You got a warrant to turn this gaff over?' I replied.

'Why, you going to contact the civil liberties?'

I went on looking at him. He took a quick gulp of whisky. I was glad to see him fighting down a splutter.

'What now?' I said. 'Will I send out for a couple of girls?'

He looked round the big room.

'Interesting. An ex-copper living all alone in a big-time swindler's gaff, wearing his boudoir outfit, playing nanny to his fish. Interesting. I heard you were doing a lot of boozing after you jacked it in. What was it, conscience or nerves?'

I wanted a cigarette but that would have told him I was jittery.

'You really think Mancini would've tried to go over the wall?' I said.

'I recognized your name on his letter. By the way, how's your old man?'

'Why, you planning to take him some grapes?'

He sipped the whisky.

'You're a fly boy, Hazell,' he said, almost sadly. 'I suppose it's bred into you. A big city fly boy. I never understood how come you were on the force. And now you're pals with the Gregorys? Kipping in Mancini's mansion? Very smooth. Gregory tells me you're an inquiry agent. What kind of business are you getting – professionally?'

'Just what you'd expect.'

'Divorce? Petty debt recovery? Missing poodles?'

'I've got a few earners. How about yourself? Found the magic password yet?'

The rapid movements of his eyelids – for Minty the equivalent of an emotional rampage – proved *that* went home. Your earners is coppers' language for pay-off money. Pay-off money is like the wind – it can come from any point of the compass and it's invisible, but you can always tell when it's happening.

Minty had always believed I was on the take.

I never was but knowing what a dour old holy joe he was, even at twenty-three, I liked to joke about it. He'd come straight from a turnip patch up there in the heather and I think he found all Londoners a bit too quick with the patter.

Then there was the business with my old man. Cops aren't supposed to have Dads like mine.

'I could do you the odd favour,' he said.

'Oh yeah?'

'Your line of work a friend on the inside could be a big help.'

'And what would I have to do to earn your brotherly love? Blow down your ear, is it?'

'Working with high-class rogues like the Gregorys you must hear things.'

'I get it. I'm your snout in the Gregorys' office and you give me free tickets for the Scotland Yard poetry circle?'

'Mutual aid,' he said, face still expressionless.

'I've been working on a good one,' I said chattily, 'this woman thinks they gave her the wrong baby in the maternity ward, now she wants her own baby back.'

'You're a fly boy, Hazell,' he said. 'Your father was a fly boy before you. We know where it got him.'

He finished the whisky and put down the glass. Then he thought about something. He picked up the glass and took it to the bar. He looked under the counter and found a dish-towel. He wiped the glass clean.

'I'll be seeing you later then,' he said. 'I'm glad to know you're holding your own.'

I saw him down to the front door. He stood on the top step.

'Oh aye,' he said, 'that reminds me, I hear your pal O'Rourke is getting things together again. I don't suppose you want me to pass on your best wishes.'

'I don't give a monkey's fuck what you do, Jock,' I said, as cheerily as possible.

He went down the path without so much as a farewell wave.

There's always a snag, that's what I always say.

I didn't let it spoil my appetite for Sunday lunch (quarter a pound of Reggie's best smoked cheese washed down by an excellent bottle of Chateau Cowjuice) but I knew Minty's visit couldn't be ignored.

He was a clever bastard and I knew from experience that once he got his hooks into you he was harder to dodge than Christmas. That's what he wanted, to get his hooks into me. All cops reserve a special nausea for smart lawyers who wangle known villains off well-deserved stretches and having a two-legged bugging device inside the offices of Venables etc would be more than useful to Minty.

I decided I'd better motor over to Haggerston and see the old man.

There's always a snag.

I felt an attack of the elbow-bends coming on.

It was six weeks two days since I'd last touched a drop, not long enough to make my throat believe we were finished with that game.

By the time I'd driven across the river the horrors were on me. I could taste that first long gulp and I could see large glasses dancing above the cars ahead. There was no point in going to see my folks in that condition.

I drove into the West End and rammed the Stag into the first vacant space. The sun was shining as I joined the queue filing into the Leicester Square cinema for the afternoon performance.

I bought a packet of salted peanuts at a price that was making millionaires out of somebody and a carton of orange juice. My ankle was throbbing and my mouth was as dry as a lizard's tit. My palms were sweating. I felt that people were staring at me.

By the time the lights went down I was in a right state and

the worst thing was, I knew exactly what I wanted and where I could get it, just five minutes' walk across Shaftesbury Avenue into Soho.

A knock on a side door, that was all it would take. Welcome home, stranger, they'd say and the first glass would be in my shaking hand and suddenly the sun would be shining for me, too.

But I didn't go for a drink. I sat there in the dark and shoved salted gold into my mouth and smoked seven fags and bought myself a plastic ice-cream and sipped my orange-style drink and watched some teenage American professor fighting off a wild bunch of Cornish yokels whose dialogue must have been rescued from Tarzan's waste-paper basket.

It was comic-cuts melodrama but it saw me through the horrors.

The sun was still shining when I came out. Tourists jammed the pavements. Droves of them drifted along Coventry Street looking for a good time they'd never find and regret next morning if they did.

I wondered if they'd believe that some of our friendly bobbies were called Minty . . .

Mum answered the door. They were now living in a ground-floor flat. The block wasn't exactly a twin of Herbert Morrison House but it wasn't mentioned a lot in Homes and Gardens. She threw her arms round my neck and then stood back, her eyes a little wet.

'Let me look at you, Jimmy. You've lost weight! You're not eating like you should.'

Through the open door of the living-room I could see the top of the old man's bald head. He didn't turn round to give me any big hallo. This was just his way of letting me know he was annoyed I hadn't been to see them for months, not since Jackie walked out. I knew he wouldn't be annoyed for long.

I was his favourite son, wasn't I?

I had to be, there were no others.

'I'll make some tea,' Mum said excitedly. 'You're not rushing off, I hope?'

'Not for five minutes.'

The old man used one of his walking sticks to press the button that switched off the telly.

'In trouble then?' he muttered, still gazing at the blank screen.

'Nope, just popped in.'

'Yer mum'll be pleased.'

'What is it with you?' I asked. I always found the rough approach best with the old man. 'You're a miserable bleeder. You've got it made, sitting here all day shouting orders to Mum . . . Gladys get the tea, Glad I'm hungry, Glad I fancy something to eat, Glad I'm . . .'

'Don't come in here breathin' all strong,' he growled. 'You come here, once every pancake day! Don't start givin' me the Perry Masons.'

'All right, I give in. You know how things are, time just gallops by.'

'Yeah well, you could pop in for Mum's sake, couldn't yer?'

'From now on, I promise.'

'That's all right, then.'

Mum came back in with the tea, Dad with his same old Coronation mug, four times the size of any normal cup. Mum disappeared back into the kitchenette.

'Choc Minty came round to visit me today,' I said.

'What did that bleeder want?'

'The old you-help-me and I'll-help-you spiel.'

'You wanna watch that berk, Jim,' he said. 'How are you supposed to help him then?'

'He hears I'm working with the Gregorys, he wants me to be his snout in the office.'

Mum came back into the room with a plate of buttered scones. Dad finished off his first while I was still chewing my first bite. He wiped his mouth with the sleeve of his old brown cardigan.

'Did your friend ask about me?'

Mum looked at us both but our faces showed nothing.

'Yeah he did, only in passing.'

'Never gives up, does he, big Scotch berk.'

'Well, Jimmy, what are you up to, being careful I hope,' said Mum. 'How's the ankle?'

'It's fine. Got a good line of work now, haven't I? The slush business, you could call it.'

'What's that?'

'The twentieth century Solomon, that's me.'

'What's he on about?' she said to Dad.

It was just something to talk about, for Mum's sake. I told her about Mrs Gunning and her fantasy about baby-switching.

'Is this going to be one of your sick jokes?' she interrupted.

'Nah – straight up! She's come all the way from California. I have to take her out to Valentine's Park yesterday, she gets a close-up of this other kid from Bethnal Green, she says it's hers. Cos the hair's the same colour!'

It was meant to be just a little yarn, something to show her I wasn't in shtuck with any dodgy business, but Mum took it seriously.

'I never heard of that before,' she said. 'But it could happen, in them big hospitals. What a terrible thing for the poor woman!'

'She's survived six years with the wrong kid,' I said, winking at Dad.

'Easy to see you ain't a mother,' she said. 'Cor, if that had happened to you and I found out about it later I'd – well, honest, I don't know what I'd be capable of, honest I don't.'

'You'd kill for me, Mum, would you?'

'All right for you to chortle, Jimmy, I know how a mother feels. She won't be able to live with herself till she gets her own baby back. I mean, if she's rich, it stands to reason she don't want her own baby brought up in that place in Bethnal Green, does she? It's horrible in Bethnal Green.'

'Garn, it's no bleedin' different than here,' growled the old man.

'That's only your opinion, innit? It wouldn't be right anyway, leaving the poor little dear here when it could be getting the best chance in the world with its proper parents. I hope you're doing your best for the poor woman, Jim.'

'Oh yeah,' bawled the old man, 'an' wot about the other kid then, the one wot's in America? They gonna swap 'em back, are they? Wot they say to the other one, just stroll up and announce, 'ere, mush, you aint our kid after all so git them posh clothes off, we're sendin' you back to your real mum and dad in a slum in London, England? Keep in touch, wonchyer?'

'I'll get some biscuits,' Mum said, looking extremely worried. As soon as she was out of the room I turned to Dad.

'Never mind all that baby crap, you know Minty told me O'Rourke's back on the scene?'

'Yeah, I heard. Don't worry about me, they done me once they aint gonna bother themselves twice. I'm just an old geezer now. You wanna watch yourself but.'

'What good's it going to do him, having me sorted out? He knows I don't have the money.'

'You never did unnerstan' what it's all about, did you, mate?' the old man said, almost pityingly.

I shrugged. I understood all too well what he meant. That's why I had the crazy idea of joining the police in the first place, to get out of it.

If you weren't brought up in the East End you might find it hard to accept but this is what happened. My old man had a lot of jobs in his time, some of them a bit dodgy but never real villainy, he says. He ended up managing this betting shop in Camden Town. One Saturday night when they were getting the day's take together for the all-night safe deposit three of them in nylon masks steam into the shop with pick-handles.

My old man isn't going to let *any* old villain take a stroll with four and a half grand so he puts up a fight. The rest of the staff just looked on while the three heavies clobbered him with the pick-handles but the old man had a lot of apple even at fifty and he puts up such a show he sees one of the team off – the other two grab the lolly and scarper.

The one who doesn't get away is called Alan O'Rourke, a cousin of the O'Rourke Minty mentioned, Keith O'Rourke, the heavy one of the family. He's then doing seven years on the Moor for attempted manslaughter.

Alan gets four years for the betting shop caper. What gets up the noses of the O'Rourkes is that his mates, Terry Harris and Albert Dawkins, keep on running with the four and a half grand, courageously deciding to hang onto Alan's share.

65

As it happens Harris and Dawkins turn up in a stolen car in Fulham, the division I'm attached to at the time. I wasn't in the car that picked them up but the coincidence is enough for the O'Rourkes.

They blame the old man for Alan's arrest and they blame me for the fact that Harris and Dawkins don't have the money. And Minty gets the idea that my old man was in on the job in the first place! Reckoning the old man had an argument about his share and decided to look good by having a go, like square punters are supposed to.

As a copper I was safe enough – the blokes who kept slamming the car door on my ankle were a team of South London heavies on a wages snatch and had no connection with the O'Rourkes – but I was on my own now.

So the state of the parties was this: My old man had his two walking sticks and his shaky hands as his reward for not letting young Alan O'Rourke walk off with the betting shop money.

Harris and Dawkins would either get a dose of cosmetic surgery in the nick or when they got out, if they decided to commit suicide by hanging about.

And now Keith O'Rourke was out of Dartmoor he might very well decide the family honour could only be upheld by blowing off my toes at the knees.

There's just one thing I've forgotten to mention. When they picked up Harris and Dawkins in a stolen car in Fulham I wasn't one of the arresting officers but I did manage to see them in the station cells, where I chided them for what they'd done to my old man.

They were entitled to a good chiding, weren't they?

They might have spread the word that I had chided them into telling where the four and a half grand was tucked away. In this world of ours people like the O'Rourkes would not be rendered speechless with shock and horror at the thought of a copper who regarded stolen property as his old-age fund.

Worrying, isn't it, that the lower orders should believe such disgusting rumours?

'Well, just watch who you open the door to,' I said to the old man.

66

'I know Keith O'Rourke, he won't be wastin' time carvin' up an old wreck like me.'

I ate enough to keep the old lady happy and promised not to stay away so long next time. At the door she caught hold of my arm, looked up into my face and said, with real worry on her face:

'You do your best for that poor woman. I'm a mother and I know what she's going through.'

When I got back to Putney the phone was ringing. It was Gordon Gregory, wanting to know why Minty had rung him with all those questions about my association with the firm.

I told him and said I'd probably have to be finding alternative accommodation. I didn't tell him that Minty wanted me to be his spy in the offices of Venables, Venables, Williams and Gregory. It would only have made him worry about my integrity.

I did start to tell him about Keith O'Rourke but Gordon had bigger things in mind than my possible election to the society of legless cyclists.

'You'll be at the office tomorrow morning, won't you?' he said. 'You're in the best position to know how the Abreys will react to – '

'The Abreys? You're not letting all this cobblers go that far – are you? I mean, string her along for a few grand yes, that's what lawyers are for, but you wouldn't actually – '

'It is not cobblers, James, whatever that may mean. It's one of the most moving human dilemmas I have ever come across. It takes us into the deepest levels of human experience – not only that, it is probably unique. We may even make legal history – '

'You may – the first qualified solicitor ever to get sent down for assault with a deadly fairytale – '

'James,' he said, almost patiently, 'there are some areas in which you have a lot to learn. Fatherhood, for example, family relationships – can't you try to put yourself in the mind of this tormented woman, a mother – '

'If I was going to put myself anywhere about Mrs Gunning it wouldn't be in her mind.'

'I'll see you in the morning. And let's not have any light-hearted jests in front of Mrs Gunning, shall we?'

'You're not quite as bad as my old mum,' I said, 'I mean, you'll at least be earning out of this fairytale.'

I went to give Reggie's colourful cannibals their grub. For five guineas an hour I would sit and listen all day to Mrs Gunning's bad dream.

But what I had to start worrying over was the chance of Minty tipping off Keith O'Rourke to where I was living.

Beneath all that steamroller subtlety that's what he had been threatening.

And Keith O'Rourke was the kind of bloke who settles petty grievances with a shotgun.

Chapter Seven

Monday morning was dull and drizzly. Good old Monday morning, it never changes.

It was half past nine and in her office on the first floor of the mews house in Kensington Dot Wilmington was pouring her first brandy and dry of the day.

A short, dumpy woman with drab fair hair, nicotine-stained fingers and a richly-pickled voice, that was Dot. She carried the day's rations of brandy in a flat flask you might have mistaken for a church hymnbook, if you remember what a hymnbook looked like.

A half bottle a day, that was Dot's prescription for the acute condition called life. She had two large ones at a time when most women of her age were decently in curlers listening to the Jimmy Young show.

'I had a visit from Choc Minty,' I said. 'He wanted me to know that Keith O'Rourke's getting busy again. You heard anything?'

'That's not my scene any more, thank God,' she said, wheezing a little as she screwed on the flask cap. 'These roughnecks don't bother my kind of client. So what else is new? How're you making out with that bastard Gregory?'

'All right, as it happens. The money's good.'

'What kind of villainy has he got going for him?'

'I dunno why you got the needle for Gordon. I'm on a job that wouldn't strain the missing collar department of Battersea Dogs Home. The wrong baby case, that's what he's paying me to crack.'

I snorted. But her female ears seized on the magic word – baby.

So I had to tell her about Mrs Gunning and the Abreys. As far as I was concerned I'd heard better on Mrs Dale's Diary but the more she listened the deeper became the lines on Dot's forehead.

Of course, she'd never had any babies of her own.

'That's terrible,' she said, shaking her head. 'And you're making a big joke out of it? And Gregory's going to take her money and then send her packing?'

'Come off it, Dot, what're you getting all worked up about? Christ, the jobs you do geezers get sent down for five-year stretches and I've never seen you spill a drop.'

She shook her head slowly, looking at me as if I was something new Doctor Frankenstein had just cooked up.

'The people I deal with ask for all they get,' she said, 'but these two families – a thing like this could ruin their whole lives. All because of a careless mistake.'

'It won't ruin their lives because they won't even know it happened.'

'She knows, doesn't she, the mother, the one from Los Angeles? The one you and Gregory are joking about?'

'Maybe she's going through the change of life. Women get funny notions then, don't they?'

'You bastard. Sometimes I think I'm getting a sick attitude to this world – you deal with villains and swindlers and conmen long enough you begin to look at this town and think – is there one living soul alive who isn't bent?'

'I'm not bent!'

'No, you're what they call a moral imbecile.'

'Thanks, is that bad?'

She started on about the mothers and the kids. But from now on I was going to keep my smalltalk to England's plans for the next World Cup. Every time I opened my mouth about this baby nonsense hearts started bleeding all over me.

'Yeah yeah,' I said when I'd had enough of her rabbiting on about the great dilemma, 'so even if it is true, what the hell could be done about it?'

'Done?' she ranted. 'There's a child's whole future at stake! Is it going to be left to rot in that dump in Bethnal Green when all the time it could be enjoying the best money can buy – with its proper parents?'

'Oh yeah, great for *her*. But what about the other one? The kid in California? As my old man said, they going to tell it there's been a slip-up so you've got to go off and live in a foreign slum? Don't worry, little girl, you can study cockney language on gramophone records, and get rid of all those proper table manners, where you're going they pick their noses and flick it round the room?'

Dot frowned.

'That's true,' she said, sounding puzzled. 'I wasn't thinking of the other child. They'd have to be swapped over, wouldn't they?'

'I'm sure I don't know. This Gunning woman will just have to go home and make do with the child she's got.'

'I wouldn't count on her doing that,' said Dot.

'What else?'

'I really don't know. I've never been a mother – don't smirk – but if it's got me agitated what's it doing to her? My God, I need another drink. You've fair spoiled my day.'

I left her sipping and pondering. As I gunned the Stag through Knightsbridge and under the Piccadilly tunnel I couldn't help smiling. She hadn't been the slightest bit interested in the fact that Keith O'Rourke was on the loose, probably planning to blow me apart. That was all in the game, wasn't it? But mention these rotten babies . . .

Mrs Gunning and Gordon were already sipping coffee from bone china cups when I followed Diane's buttocks into Gordon's office. I was three minutes early but I had the impression they'd been chatting for some time.

She nodded to me without a smile.

I was wrong about one thing, I thought, taking a low-level chair at the other end of Gordon's desk. Nobody with a body and legs like hers was going through the change.

If she was, the old model must have been something else.

Her eyes had lost all their puffiness. She looked fairly stunning, handsome rather than beautiful, and I couldn't help thinking that for two women from the same background she'd drawn a better hand than Toni Abrey. ·

We waited till the office junior, one of the new fifteen-year-olds with the shy, girlish charm of a traffic warden, shoved my coffee through the door, which she then took care to slam.

Behind his big desk, Gordon sat back in his chair, straightened his blotter pad, cleared his throat and wriggled his exquisite shoulders.

'I must start by saying this isn't the kind of legal situation I have much experience of,' he began. 'However, that may be an advantage, fresh viewpoint and so on.'

It was easy to make the mistake of dismissing Gordon as a lightweight – and not just because he was thinner than a pound-note at a slimming farm. He had a baby-face complexion and curly brown hair and his movements were languid to the point of being disjointed and his accent was so posh it sounded like a Monty Python parody of the old Etonian nit.

But this was his territory and he was about as satirical as Murder Incorporated.

'Before we get involved in the technicalities, Mrs Gunning – this could be important – you didn't do or say anything in the park on Saturday which could prejudice whatever steps we intend to take, did you?'

'I don't think so. I only spoke to the two little girls – Patricia's friend had dropped her ice-cream and the Abreys were quite far away. I didn't say who I was.'

'What did you say?'

'I said what lovely dresses they were wearing and then I gave the other child some money to buy another ice-cream. That was all. As soon as I saw him approaching I just walked away. Was that wrong?'

'No, I'm just being cautious, lawyer's failing,' he said with a smile that came and went as fast as a happy day. 'Now let me sum up your situation, Mrs Gunning. You have a child in California who, the evidence of blood tests seems to indicate, is not the child you gave birth to. The only time your child could possibly have been switched with somebody else's child was in the hospital, immediately after delivery. We know that another woman in the same maternity ward also gave birth to a baby girl on the same day. You have seen this other child and you are convinced – '

He stopped and gave her a long look. I liked the cool, dry way he was laying it on the line.

' – yes, convinced,' she said, 'as certain as I am of my own existence. I'm not suggesting our flesh called out to each other – but I *knew*, looking at her in the park, I just knew. We've very much alike, you know.'

'You're convinced that this child, Patricia Abrey, bears a strong physical resemblance to yourself, the colour of her hair and so on. You have also seen Clifford Abrey and you suggest there's an equally strong resemblance between him and your child, I mean Helen. The child you brought up as your own. And now, I take it, you wish to explore the possibility of having your own child, that is, Patricia Abrey, restored to you and your husband as her actual parents?'

'I want my baby, yes,' she said, her voice firmly under control.

'The legal position, then, would seem to be this: First you would have to prove – or at least produce a substantial body of evidence to indicate that Patricia Abrey is, in fact, your child. The onus of proof will definitely be on you. You would probably need a court order to make the Abreys subject their child to blood tests.'

'Blood tests are only negative evidence anyway,' I said, 'they only show who is *not* the father or mother of a particular child.'

'It's a bit more complicated. There are at least fourteen groups. Certain things occur only one in a million times. If we were very lucky the tests might just conceivably show that Mrs Gunning and her husband are almost certainly the child's true parents. Now, presuming the blood tests showed that the Abreys were not Patricia's natural parents – and that they could, in fact be the parents of your little girl, ehm – '

'Helen.'

'Yes, Helen, then that would go a long way to establishing that part of your case. We would then have to show how the

73

babies were erroneously named by the hospital staff. It isn't impossible, there was a case in Buckinghamshire quite recently, the mothers spotted it instantly but the hospital was only convinced after blood tests. We'd have to show evidence of general carelessness, over-work, under-staffing, in other words we'd have to make a pretty strong case against the efficiency of the hospital administration. I think we can rule out the possibility of the mistaken identification being deliberate and there – '

'Just a minute,' said Mrs Gunning.

I sat up. It had come to me at exactly the same moment, something my memory had dragged up from that first conversation with Toni and Cliff.

It was an eerie sensation, knowing what she was going to say before the words reached my ears.

'I don't think you should rule it out,' she said, 'there was a nurse I kept having rows with. She was an old witch – we all thought she drank, on duty.'

Gordon looked at me.

'Yeah,' I said reluctantly, regretting that I'd shown any reaction, 'Mrs Abrey mentioned the same nurse. Her name was – '

'Drummond!' exclaimed Mrs Gunning.

We looked at each other. Her eyes were a light shade of grey. At that moment they were shining with honesty, no other word for it. She just couldn't be that good an actress.

'Did this nurse ever say anything that could suggest she disliked you *that* much?' Gordon asked, frowning with disbelief.

'You know what one of our rows was about? Right after the delivery, when I came round, back in the ward, I asked to see my baby, Drummond said I had to wait for the night nurse! Can you imagine – making a mother wait to see her baby because she was going off duty?'

If it was a performance they were sharing out the Oscars among the wrong people. Gone was the snappy, loudmouth neurotic. This was a mother, fighting for her baby, for her very life. The fact that I was impressed made me want to spit.

'And was it Nurse Drummond who eventually brought the baby to you in the ward?' Gordon asked.

'No, I had to wait half an hour till the night nurse came on duty.'

'Mmmm.' Gordon poked at the papers on his desk. Then he wriggled his shoulders and resumed his masterly face. 'At least that puts her in a position to have – however, let's stick to the general position. Supposing we can show the strong probability of the two babies having been wrongly identified, one way or the other, that brings us to the third, and most formidable stage.'

He held up some sheets of paper, stapled together at the corner.

'There is a precedent – of sorts,' he said. 'This is from the Weekly Law Reports, March, sixty-nine. I'll give you the gist of it. A Spanish couple were living in England and when the mother fell ill they put their young son in the care of foster-parents. He lived with them for about a year, then the parents took him back to Spain. He fell ill and after about seventeen months they decided his health would be improved by sending him back to the foster-parents in England. He was about eight then.

'When the real parents wanted him back, the foster-parents said they wanted to keep him. He was made a ward of court. It came to a hearing about two years later, when the boy was ten. The judge ordered that care and control be committed to the foster-parents, although the boy was to be brought up in the Catholic faith and to be told who his real parents were.'

Gordon looked up.

'I'm with you so far,' said Mrs Gunning.

I was glad of that. Was I the only man alive who found babies less thrilling as a topic than tariff barriers? Seeing to Keith O'Rourke over flashing meathooks was going to be a picnic after this.

Gordon went on.

'When the foster-parents went to court to ask permission to bring the boy up in the Church of England the Spanish couple decided to sue again for his return. They now had a modern house, the father had a good job and the mother's health was back to normal. No argument about it, they were entirely fit and capable of having him back. However – and I quote – there was medical evidence that in view of his relationship with his foster parents as parental figures, and with other members of the family, the chances that he would make a successful adjustment in Spain were slight – and that if he did not the consequences for his future emotional stability and happiness were grave.

'The judge accepted as a general proposition that it was for the welfare of a child to be in the hands of unimpeachable parents and were it not for the dangers of adjustment to life in Spain would have made the order for which the parents asked, but he considered there was no reasonable chance of such adjustment and that a return to Spain would be disastrous for the infant ... he turned the Spanish couple down. So did the Court of Appeal. That's when it reached the Lords.'

He stopped there.

'Shall I have the girl bring in more of our execrable office coffee?'

'Don't worry about me,' said Mrs Gunning, 'I'll listen to this all day and night if it's going to help me get my child back.'

I was nodding eagerly in favour of more coffee but Gordon refused to catch my eye. I was smoking a lot and my mouth was as dry as a buzzard's crotch. I even raised my hand a little but he ignored me.

'The Lords started off by holding that the case came under the Guardianship of Infants Act, 1925, the point being that the court shall at all times put the welfare of the child as first and paramount consideration. One of their Lordships said that serious harm may be caused to even young children by a change in custody. It was also said that although the rights and wishes of the parents must preponderate in many cases, they were not absolute.

'That might sound bad from your point of view, Mrs Gunning, but a key point I've taken from their Lordships was that their decision might have been different if the Spanish boy had been only five, instead of ten.

'I take that to mean that a younger child might not be harmed so much by a change in environment. And, of course, the court might take the view that America is a somewhat more desirable alternative environment than Spain – '

He smiled.

'At least it would be easier to learn the lingo,' I said.

They both gave me sharp looks but found no objectionable smile on my face.

'Two good points from our point of view,' Gordon went on. 'The Act applies to strangers – that is, citizens of a foreign country – '

'Oh we're still British,' said Mrs Gunning. 'I'm travelling on my British passport.'

'Jolly good. Dollars can't buy everything, eh?'

'Only in America,' I murmured. When they glanced at me I pretended to be clearing my throat. It wasn't too painful as long as I kept repeating the magic formula, five guineas an hour.

'The other good thing is that this decision is only likely to be followed in very exceptional circumstances. In other words, where all else is equal the natural parents come first.'

We all knew where that took us. All else was not equal to the tune of a million dollars or so.

'I take it, Mrs Gunning, you'll claim that because of your position you can give this child a much better home background, education and so on, than the Abreys?'

'Too damn right I'll claim it,' she said. It hadn't struck me before but for this meeting she was using her American voice. 'You had a look at where the Abreys live?'

'And you'll have no objection to the point being made forcibly that you are, in comparison, tolerably well off?'

'We're stinking rich if that's what you mean. Is it a crime?' Gordon laughed.

'Not yet. To be stinking rich is still a great help in most matters. It makes certain, however, that you won't get Legal Aid for any court proceedings. The Abreys will certainly qualify on grounds of low income so they won't be under any disadvantage on that score. And I must warn you that proceedings would be expensive, Mrs Gunning, you – '

'I'm not worried about the cost.'

'Contrary to popular belief I always, as a solicitor, advise clients to stay out of court where humanly possible,' said Gordon. 'What we have to consider are the other options open to us. James, you're the one who knows the Abreys best, what's their reaction likely to be?'

'You mean, if we arrive on the doorstep and tell them Mrs Gunning here wants the kid back so get its clothes packed?'

'It's just his manner,' he said to Mrs Gunning, apologetically.

'Cliff Abrey only lives for that kid, that's all,' I said, airily. 'He doesn't drink, smoke, work overtime or support a football team – all for Tricia's sake. He won't let the wife have any more kids in case they deprive darling Trish of the good things in life, like clothes, ice-creams, plastic toys, colour TV. He doesn't let her play round the block in case she hears rude words. You could call him a fairly doting father. How would he react? I should think the lucky bastard who turns up with all this good news will get a right royal welcome.'

An Eton accent doesn't necessarily mean the guy is a noddy.

'You haven't said anything about Mrs Abrey,' said Gordon, fixing me with his boyish minces.

No, I hadn't and suddenly it looked very obvious.

'She's an average East End housewife type,' I shrugged.

'But how would she react?'

'I only spoke to them for half an hour,' I said, indignantly. 'I was supposed to be researching a TV programme about the hospital. It's not the first stray question that comes to mind, is it, what's your feelings on having your saucepan lid confiscated by a total stranger?'

'No,' said Gordon slowly, 'yet you're very definite about the father. Still, that's not crucial at this stage. Let's assume we're in court. We've been able to show that Patricia Abrey is almost certainly the child Mrs Gunning gave birth to in St Margaret's. Now we have to prove it's in the child's best interests to be taken away from the Abreys, taken away from the only environment she knows and sent off to a foreign country to parents she's never heard of. Both sides will call psychologists and social workers to prove entirely different conclusions. You can give the child every material advantage known to man – but the Abreys are the parents she knows and presumably loves.

You live in a paradise compared to Bethnal Green – but is an English judge going to rule that a working-class home, even in Bethnal Green, is so obnoxious as to be good reason for sending an English child to a foreign country?'

Gordon stood up. He leaned forward, both hands splayed on his desk-blotter, his sharp young face telling us about the seriousness of it all.

'A hearing like that would go pretty deeply into the respective circumstances of both families, Mrs Gunning. Your money isn't in doubt – but what about your morals? If I'm the typical English judge I am looking at you and thinking all sorts of puritanical thoughts about the pop music industry – drugs, sex orgies, broken marriages. Are you – '

'I get the picture,' she said dryly.

'It'll go deep, you know. You'll be battling on more than purely legal grounds, all sorts of innate prejudices will – '

'But you said we didn't want to go to court only as a last resort,' she said. 'So what other ways can we try first?'

'I've had thoughts in that direction.'

Gordon came round the end of his desk and stood beside my chair. My ankle was throbbing again. It's not too hysterical about babies either. I leaned forward to give it a bit of a rub. My face was only a few inches away from Gordon's feet. I had the peculiar thought that he was actually a very short man on stilts. I mean, I've never seen such thin ankles.

While I was down there I had a gander at Mrs Gunning's nyloned scotches. If she was on stilts I'd be a carpenter.

None of this is important but I thought I'd better explain why my face was at ankle-level and my brain somewhere else.

'Good taste makes it repugnant for me to say it out loud, Mrs Gunning, but your money will probably be our best weapon. Without being cynical – well, you know what I mean.'

He went back round his desk and sat there, thin elbows resting on shiny wood.

'So? What now?' she asked.

'We'll deal with it in stages,' said Gordon. 'James I want you to get started on the hospital. You know what we need – evidence of administrative slip-ups, carelessness among the staff.

You might start by making a friend of this Nurse – Drummond? I can't find it easy to believe a nurse would go against every principle of her profession – but we do know she was on duty at the crucial time. Anyway, she'll probably be a rich repository of all hospital gossip. She may give you some leads. If we can prove that hospital was being run like Fred Karno's army then – you know what's wanted, James.'

I gathered I was being told to leave the room. I should have taken the hint and made a rush for the door.

'Okay,' I said, not getting out of the chair, 'just out of interest, however, you've been talking a lot about how this affects Patricia Abrey. How's it going to go down with your own kid, Mrs Gunning? Helen, I mean. None of my business, maybe, but does she know she's up for swaps?'

Maybe I just wanted something I could tell my Mum and Dot to ease their great big bleeding hearts.

Just for a moment there was a silence in that room you could have put in bottles and flogged to people with tense ears.

Next moment it was broken by the unmistakable sound of the other thing women are good at. Dragging a handkerchief from her white handbag the tough, rich, handsome Mrs Gunning was crying her eyes out.

Surprise, surprise.

'Oh my God, oh my God,' she kept sobbing.

From the glare Gordon gave me I took it he was nominating me for the Supershit hall of fame.

As I left the room he was standing over her, one long thin hand touching her shoulder. Did I have a dirty mind or was he taking too warm a grip for mere comfort?

Chapter Eight

'Are you out of your bloody mind?'

Pulling my eyes off Gordon's secretary I turned, the telephone at my ear. Gordon's features were not designed for primitive emotions, which made his temper all the more frightening. If you were easily frightened.

I put my hand over the mouthpiece.

'You speaking to me?' I said pleasantly.

At the other end of the line they were fetching the secretary of St Margaret's.

Gordon caught his girl's eye and his face went red. He motioned for me to step out into the corridor. I heard a voice at the other end of the line.

'Hello, Mr Greenfield, this is James Hazell of Venables . . .

Mr Greenfield remembered my letter about Mrs Abrey.

'See me before you go,' Gordon hissed in my ear. He went back to his office to apply more emotional first aid to Mrs Gunning. I gave Diane a bold wink. She was wearing one of those new old-fashioned blouses that cover everything but hide nothing. Her lips tightened as if she thought an outright smile would be bad form.

I enjoyed watching her well-educated face as I explained my new line of enquiry to Mr Greenfield of St Margaret's.

Remember my Boy Scout notions about telling lies?

At five guineas an hour who's got time these days to light fires by rubbing sticks?

'We've contacted Mrs Abrey,' I said, 'our client is very grateful for your help. What she wants now is to contact a nurse on your staff – Drummond is the name.'

I didn't actually tell any direct lies but if Mr Greenfield got the impression that our client in faraway America wanted to remember, in tangible form, the gruff but kindly old nurse who had looked after her all those years ago he didn't get it from Harold Wilson. Wasn't it heart-warming, in these callous, self-seeking times, to come across someone who *remembered*?

Mr Greenfield said he would be delighted to check the staff lists and phone me back. I put down the phone.

Diane gazed up at me, shaking her well-bred head.

'Good, was I?' I said.

'You convinced me and I *knew* you were fibbing,' she said. She had one of those soopah accents. Fibbing, indeed.

'You should hear me when I'm coming clean,' I said. 'How about a few drinks and some real lies over dinner?'

'I wouldn't know when to believe you.'

'Oh yes you would – when it was too late to do anything about it.'

She *giggled*. Soopah.

Gordon reappeared. He nodded for me to follow him out into the corridor and then into the gents. We stood beside the basins.

'You wouldn't make a good lawyer, James,' he said, his bad temper forgotten. 'We do not allow ourselves the profitless luxury of emotional involvement.'

Standing between all those mirrors I couldn't escape the fact of how tall he was. It was irritating. I moved back against a basin and rested one hip on the edge.

'I couldn't give bananas, mate,' I said, 'but that story of hers? Dreamtime! You actually see these kids being swapped over?'

'There's a long way to go before that,' he said. He smirked meaningfully. I didn't know what meaning I was supposed to take.

'You can swap over the Dagenham girl pipers for all I care,' I said, 'I've got bigger things to occupy me. You know Keith O'Rourke's back in London and he's saying he's going to mark my card? You can put every baby in bleeding Britain up for a raffle as far as I'm concerned. I just thought it was worth mentioning, that's all. If she's got no hope let's cut the cackle and –'

'There's always hope, James.'

'I don't mind taking five guineas an hour off you but what's the point of flogging our guts out – my guts anyway – if all the time – '

He was smirking again. This time I got it.

'Go through the motions?' I said.

He nodded.

'You cynical bastard,' I said.

He actually smiled.

So I hung about the office making smart patter for Diane's benefit until my friend Mr Greenfield phoned back.

'Kathleen Drummond,' he said. 'She's the one your client must mean, a midwifery nurse. I'm afraid she's no longer with us.'

'Gone to another hospital, has she?'

'I don't think so.'

'Retired, I suppose, at her age.'

'She left here – let me see – oh yes – nineteen sixty-nine, August twentieth. I can give you an address.'

I got into the Stag and drove off along Holborn towards the mysterious East End – again.

As I went into Newgate Street it started to rain. I put the radio on. The BBC disc jockey was the usual Australian with the American touch. Or maybe he was a Canadian whose mother came from Galway Bay. His patter was brisk and monotonous. The records all sounded the same. I used to like pop music when the Beatles and Rolling Stones were big. Maybe I was getting old. I switched off the radio and switched on the windscreen wipers. At least they made a noise I could hum to.

At the Mile End address the hospital had given me a small, cheery woman in an apron and headscarf asked me in out of the drizzle while she poked around for a piece of paper on which she had Kathleen Drummond's forwarding address.

'You ain't the law you said?' she prattled as she started open-cast mining in sideboard drawers. 'I mean I'd a bellyful of that Drummond but I wouldn't wish no 'arm to her, would I? When I 'ad her as a lodger I fort she was still up in the 'ospital, didn't I? Only she was gettin' the elbow, wunt she? I'm surprised she ever 'eld a job like that, wiv her drinkin' an' that. Proper old guzzler she were! An' temper! I told her in the end, didn't I, after they give her the elbow, you'll 'ave to go, mate, I says, I like a drop of somefink myself but not that much. A nurse? Good luck I weren't one of her patients! Makes you laff, dunnit? A nurse – comin' back 'ere all hours singin' and shoutin'? Oh yeah, 'ere it is, luv, I wrote it down, why I bovvered I don't know. You aint the law you said?'

'No, it's solicitors,' I said.

'That's all right then, innit?'

I left that little wet street of terraced doll's houses and drove to the next address, in Stepney Green, on the north side of Commercial Road.

This one turned out to be a hostel for single women. Nobody seemed particularly interested in why I was looking for Drummond. The assistant warden looked up her book and told me Kathleen Drummond had been a resident from November, sixty-nine, until March, seventy.

She had been asked to leave the hostel as a result of persistent drunkenness. During one incident the police had been called.

'I remember her now,' said the lady warden, 'lonely, of course – but then they all are to some extent. She'd spend day after day in total silence, wouldn't speak to a soul, and then she'd go off on a bout when she collected her pension. In drink I'm afraid she was very troublesome, abusing the staff, fighting with the other women. Of course, one gets used to it, one has to, but it always seems more degrading in an older woman. I think she was basically very lonely.'

There was a forwarding address care of a Mr W. J. Drummond in Millwall.

I thanked the lady and checked the Millwall address in my A to Z streetmap. I then drove through the rain, along Ben Johnson Road once again into West India Dock Road and then along West Ferry Road into the Isle of Dogs.

I've heard it said the name goes back to Henry the Eighth. He was supposed to have kept his hunting pack there. It isn't an island, it sticks into the Thames and is cut off from the outside by the West India Docks. Maybe Henry liked it there, to get away from the wife screaming her head off.

As I guessed, Mr W. J. Drummond was a relative of Nurse Drummond. However, he wasn't much help. He was dead.

'He was taken in May last year,' the Irish woman next door told me. 'I shouldn't speak ill of nobody but it was her carryings on dat worried him into his grave. I wish no harm on nobody but if she's in trouble I wouldn't be surprised. I tink she'd been a nurse. Imagine dat! Poor Mr Drummond, he lived clean, you know what I mean? What a nice man he was. He didn't want her here, he told me dat himself, but what could he do, her being his only living relation?'

'Do you happen to know where she went after he died?'

'Once she got de insurance money she just left. She owed for the rent, electric, gas – dey've all been here and tried to find her but dey says she's just disappeared.'

'You wouldn't know what insurance company Mr Drummond dealt with?'

'He wouldn't tell me dat, would he now?'

The trail of the lonely ex-nurse who went on drinking bouts seemed to end there, on the Isle of Dogs. It was just after two o'clock.

I found a small café among the warehouses and sheds and had a bacon sandwich and a cup of tea. Experts had been on TV warning the nation about water-rationing if the freak dry-spell kept up but through the steamy café window I saw enough rain to top up the Atlantic.

Where else should I try? Kathleen Drummond was drawing a state pension so her current whereabouts were known to some computer somewhere. That kind of information is supposed to be highly confidential but there are ways.

Only I wasn't going to risk a gaol sentence. Gordon had made it pretty clear. We were just going through the motions. The only thing Mrs Gunning was going to get custody of from my efforts was a cuddly little bouncing bill.

The door of the café banged open. The man who came in had red hair. Just for a moment I tensed up. He stood at the counter with his back to me. He was wearing a black donkey jacket.

Then he turned and I gave a little soundless whistle of relief. It wasn't Keith O'Rourke. Looked like him though, for a prickly moment.

Something would have to be done about that geezer. I

couldn't be spending the rest of my natural doing little jumps when red-haired men came through the door.

Just to cover all angles I found a callbox and phoned the *East London Press* number. The reporter I asked for, Fred Parkes, was not in. I left a message for him to call me at Dot Wilmington's number and then I drove back through the City towards Kensington.

When I turned into the mews a guy in a Jag was just pulling out. I backed a few yards to let him past. Before I could move forward again another geezer in a Rover shot past me, stopped just past the vacant space and started to back in.

I gave him a blast on the horn and rammed the Stag forward nose first into the empty space.

'Where the bloody hell you think you're going?' he bawled out of his window.

'I was here first,' I shouted back.

'Were you fuck!'

I opened the door and got out, putting on my cheery heavy-merchant's face.

He revved up the Rover and shot down to the far end of the mews. I got back into the Stag and pushed her forward. Then I reversed into the empty space. He came back up the mews, backwards. I stood at the front of the Stag and waited.

He said nothing until his tail-end was turning into the street. Then he rolled down his window again and shouted some obscene threat or another.

'Yeah, all right,' I yelled back, starting to walk up that way. He got the Rover into the street and shot off.

It's what they call the community spirit.

'Any messages?' I said, standing in the doorway of Maureen's office on the first floor.

'Dot wants to see you.'

It sounded too much like an order.

'Tell her I'm upstairs,' I said. 'You got a typewriter I can borrow?'

'No. You'll have to buy one, won't you?'

I shrugged. I felt weary as I climbed the stairs. My trousers were damp and my cubby-hole smelled of wet cloth and yesterday's smoke. The carpet wasn't too fragrant either. I sat down and lit a cigarette. Rag Trade Reggie's fishy letter was still the only thing in my wire basket.

'What's it all about?' I said out loud. 'Come on, Jim-Jim, keep moving.'

I had just enough energy to sit there and stare straight ahead. On that wall was a big colour map of London. Maybe one of Dot's operatives had fancied himself sticking flags in it to represent the scenes of his triumphs. It was a nice map, blue for the Thames, light green for the parks, yellow for the main roads. London Town was a very big spread. Maybe that was why I was feeling tired. Never mind travelling all over it, just to look at that big map made me feel *lost*. Nobody could make sense of it all. Maybe we weren't meant to. It had everything, parks, cemeteries, houses, churches, schools but the one thing it didn't show was people. How would you show people on a map? Dots? They'd be so small they'd be invisible. Nurse Kathleen Drummond was up there, just one invisible dot among the nice colours. Toni Abrey was up there, a dot coming out of Herbert Morrison House in the rain, going along the street in the rain to fetch her little girl home from school. Rag Trade Reggie was off the map for the while, a missing dot the map wouldn't even notice. There wasn't one place called London Town, there were a thousand different worlds served by buses of the same colour. I didn't know a tenth of it yet look at the different worlds my dot had been moving through. Herbert Morrison House. The ritzy offices of Venables etc in High Holborn. A few inches west and Georgina Gunning was sitting in her suite in Claridges. Another dot, another world. Thousands of different worlds and millions of invisible dots . . .

The phone rang. For a moment I stared at it, surprised that it even knew of my existence.

It was Fred Parkes. I'd known him vaguely for years, since school. Keith O'Rourke had been at that school as well. Fred and I couldn't be called friends but when you looked at the size of that map on the wall you knew it was all you could hope for. To know a few of the other dots. Otherwise you might as well not exist at all.

We brought each other up-to-date on our trivialities. Fred now had five kids. My wife had left me. Fred was being buggered about by his editor. I was doing so-so as an inquiry agent. We said we must get together over a few lagers and talk about the good old happy days. Make a night of it.

'Look forward to that,' I said. 'By the way, maybe this is something could do you a bit of good. I met this TV bloke the other night at a morry, he was asking if I knew any good hospital stories.'

'Jokes and that?'

'Nah, he wants scandal – dirt.'

'What – bacteria in the cocoa? Sex orgies in the mortuary?'

'Slip-ups, people getting the wrong leg amputated, you know the kind of stuff. I seemed to remember something like that about St Margaret's. He said that was exactly the kind of hospital he wanted to cover, those old dumps. What was that story about St Margaret's again?'

'Far as I can remember we've only ever run one knocking-story about St Margaret's, about three year ago, this geezer gets run over in the street about fifty yards from the main entrance but they don't allow the casualty ward staff to fetch him in so he has to lie there in the gutter for twenty minutes till they fetch an ambulance to take him to Mile End. He didn't snuff so it didn't get much coverage in the nationals.'

'Pity. Still, you can't win 'em all. I'll get this TV guy to ring you, will I?'

'Yeah, sure. What programme was it for?'

'Blowed if I can remember. I've got his number somewhere. I'll give him a buzz.'

'I could do with some of that lovely television loot. Christ, if I was ten year younger that's where I'd be, television. This game is clapped out.'

'Yeah, I'll bet you're coining it in. Anyway, could you do me a favour?'

'Oh yeah? You don't just want to talk about the good old days then?'

'No catch, straight up. You heard anything about Keith O'Rourke?'

'Ain't he still in the nick?'

'No, I hear he's back in business. If you were to hear anything like where he's hanging out maybe you could tip me the wink, eh?'

'Leave me out! I don't want to get involved with that berk, do I?'

'You won't get involved. Don't panic. I'm planning a school re-union.'

'Don't invite me, please.'

'I just want to know where he's at. Okay?'

'Yeah, okay.'

'Ta. I'll be in touch.'

'Yeah, we must have a night on it.'

'Yeah, sure.'

I put down the phone and reached for the cigarette packet. These French smokes might be healthy but they were giving me a mouth like a bearskin rug. I lit one anyway. Funny thing, I thought, I never really liked Fred Parkes too much. I wouldn't be in touch with him again, unless he could give me some help. Isn't that what friends are for?

I pushed my chair back a few inches until it touched the wall. When Dot Wilmington came in the room was hazy with smoke and my feet were propped on a half-open drawer.

'How's the cradle-snatching business then?' Dot said, coughing wheezily. She was carrying her flask and one glass.

'It's died on us. Can't be made to stand up.'

'I'm glad to hear it. That poor woman.'

'Which woman do you mean?'

'The mother, of course, the one in Bethnal Green.'

'I thought last time you were more agitated about the other one. Or was it the kid?'

'I've been thinking about it ever since. What a terrible shock for that poor woman and her husband! They're the ones who would suffer most.'

'You getting soft in your old age? I saw in the paper that your car-park chummy got four years. You getting a cut from the company for what you've saved them?'

She perched herself on the edge of my desk and poured herself the last knocking of the day's brandy quota.

'I'd offer you a chair only I'm sitting in it,' I said.

'I had to be in court for the sentencing,' she said, unusually subdued, one leg swinging backwards and forwards. Her kneecap was a trifle podgy for my taste. 'It always depresses me. All he made out of that fiddle was twenty quid a week. Pathetic – he got a secondhand car and a cheap cruise out of it and now he's doing four years. Why do they do it?'

'To pay for cheap cruises. How did you put the finger on him? Slipped one of your blokes in as an attendant, did you? If you need anybody for that kind of work don't forget Jim, will you? I'm finding this high-level baby stuff a big hard to take.'

'I've got one coming up in Birmingham,' she said, taking a sip of brandy and dry. 'You any good at book-keeping? This big builder thinks one of his staff is leaking. He puts in his tender for the big council jobs and somehow the competition always manages to underprice him by a few hundred or so. You'd go in as a wages clerk and keep your ears flapping.'

'How long would it take?'

'Month, maybe two.'

'How much?'

'Tenner a day and exes.'

'I'm getting five guineas an hour from Gordon Gregory. I don't want to be cutting my money, Christ, I'm still young enough to hope the best times are still to come.'

'Sorry to disillusion you but you've already had them. Tell me more about the babies.'

'Leave me out! What is it about babies? She can't prove they were switched over so now she'll just have to go home and everybody can go on living happily ever after in Bethnal Green and Beverly Hills, as the case may be.'

'It's going to nag at me for ever. I just can't decide what would be the best solution.'

'That's why we pay judges so handsomely. They aint so clever but they make up their minds quickly.'

'Doesn't it get to you at all?'

'Yeah, in the neck. There is no answer.'

'There has to be.'

'All right, you're the judge. On one hand the Gunnings, rich, pushy, show-biz types. On the other hand the Abreys, not exactly poor but struggling. Along comes the fairy godmother to say that little Patricia Abrey is not really an under-privileged kid in a high-rise dump where the playground's a battleground for gangs of bother boys. No – little Patricia is a changeling, says the fairy godmother, her real parents are the beautiful rich people who live all the way across the sea in the sunshine. So, we agree to let her be yanked off to paradise? After all, you don't want to be the one who comes along in ten years' time when she's learned just enough reading and writing at an educational slum to pass as a shop assistant and say – the fairy godmother wanted to cart you off to the land of milk and honey but we told her to piss off. Fine. But that's not the whole story. If Patricia becomes a princess then the other kid, Helen, has to become a peasant. So you want to be the one who tells her about the new delights of Herbert Morrison House all those thousands of miles across the sea? Give me an honest car-park swindle any time.'

'You're sure are you? That it's not going any farther? Does this Mrs Gunning know?'

'She will tomorrow if I can borrow one of your typewriters and do an impressively worded report that will justify the hefty fee Gordon Gregory is going to lob in her lap.'

'Ask Maureen.'

With an abrupt movement she slid off my desk and went to the door. Then she stopped. She turned back, a small woman with the cheeks of a country girl and the voice of a saloon-bar major.

'If that woman really is the mother I wouldn't count on her giving up too easily,' she said. 'I wouldn't.'

I shrugged.

'It's just wages to you, isn't it?' she said.

'You want me to turn on all tear ducts? My baby, my life! Thousands of kids die every day in the great big hungry world. So what does it matter if a couple happen to have the wrong mummy? I'll let you know if I fancy that Birmingham job.'

'I don't like being hard,' she said, 'but I'm a fat, ugly woman of forty-seven with unnatural sex urges and no family. What's your excuse?'

She slammed the door!

For want of anything better I shrugged.

The phone rang.

Out there, outside this smoky little room, through the window with the rain streaming down, the invisible dots had been moving, the dots that don't show on the map with the nice colours. This was the dot called Toni.

Just as I had imagined, she had been out in the rain to collect her little girl from the primary school. Coming back from the school she had spotted a familiar face.

That's right. Kathleen Drummond, the nurse with the curse!

Chapter Nine

It wasn't really important to Toni, not then, but it gave her an excuse to phone lover-boy. Was I intending to drop by in the morning she asked, shyly.

'It's more information,' she said, giggling slightly. 'You're still keen on *information* aren't you – Jimmy?'

'Could be.'

'Playing hard to get? Only I've actually got some information. I was just bringing Tricia home – and guess who we saw? That awful nurse I was telling you about – from the maternity? She'd be good for your programme, wouldn't she? Remember I told you she lived near here?'

'So you did,' I said, 'and I'd forgotten.'

My palm felt sweaty against the phone. I changed hands and wiped the damp palm on my trousers.

'I can even give you her address, if you call round,' she said, archly.

'Give me it now, eh?'

'Oh yeah, then you won't need to bother climbing all those stairs to see boring old me? Charming, I'm sure.'

'I'll be up to see you, don't fret.'

'Promise? Anyway, they've got the lift working again so it won't exhaust you, poor old thing.' She giggled. 'You think the exercise is good for your knees?'

I was saved from answering that by the pips.

'I don't have any more change,' she shouted above them, 'it's twelve Whitnell Street, just near here. You will be coming, won't you?'

She didn't need to shout the last bit because the pips had stopped.

'Yeah, I'll be there,' I said but we had been cut off.

I was only going to see Nurse Drummond to make my report look even better, I kept telling myself.

Of course it was eerie, Toni phoning like that but it couldn't lead to anything. Even if those damned brats had been given the wrong name-tags in the hospital all those years ago nobody could ever prove it.

The BBC forecast on Reggie's radio that morning had promised sunshine and high temperatures for London. They were right about the temperatures. By the time I was in the Stag and headed once again to Bethnal Green the sky overhead was the same colour as the slate-roofs.

Thunderclaps boomed like bombs over the City. I don't like thunder and lightning. I've read that Nature releases more physical energy in one thunderstorm than all our nuclear explosions put together. I tried to console myself with the hope that we'd soon catch up. Then thunderstorms won't seem so fantastic.

The lightning made the big dark bank buildings seem like a brilliant, silvery stage set.

I got caught in a hold-up at Aldgate and sat behind steamy glass watching rain spatter white off the car in front. The engine turned over quietly and the windscreen wipers clicked in slow-time as they scythed through the rippling curtain.

Through the condensation and the bucketing rain the buses looked like red elephants plodding across shallow water.

I knew this wasn't important but I still felt tense. I told myself it was the lightning.

I checked the A to Z for Whitnell Street. It was a dead-end that ran off Fotheringham Street, which in turn led from Grange Road. To get there I would have to drive past Herbert's house.

Like most men I do daft things in the privacy of my car. The kind of things our fathers did in their little garden sheds and pigeon lofts. Like my imitations of Tony Bennett, Tom Jones, Billy Eckstine. My way they all sounded like Tommy Cooper.

'It's five guineas an hour and half the world is starving to death so keep moving, Jim-Jim,' was about the most sensible thing I told me . . .

I drove up Whitnell Street. The houses were terraced, two-storeyed, old brown brick fronted by a yard of concrete and then a low brick wall. The yard of concrete was a kind of joke garden. It only grew dustbins. Over the little roofs I could see the rectangular honeycombs of the high-rise blocks. The old poverty was nothing to get romantic about but at least the houses didn't remind you that we're all just invisible dots on that great big map. The rain had stopped. On the other side of the street, two Pakistanis were repairing a dirty old Hillman Minx, one on his back under the car, the other handing him tools from an oily cloth spread out on the pavement.

Several of the houses were empty, the windows sealed by grey sheets of corrugated iron. There was neither bell nor knocker on the front door of Number Twelve. I gave the paintwork a bang with the knuckles of my right hand.

I heard an angry woman's voice and the sound of a door slamming. Then silence. I stood back to see if there was any life at the upstairs windows.

I gave the door another pounding. Somebody was moving in there. Then the door opened just enough to let me see the head of a very old woman whose skull was like a big egg delicately outlined by a white fuzz. She had her hand over her eyes to shield them from the light. Behind her the house was dark. A thin, nauseating stench of such intensity it made me step back came wafting out into the wet street.

'Does Kathleen Drummond live here?' I said, sounding like a copper. It was one imitation I did well.

'Who's that?' mumbled the old woman.

'I understand Kathleen Drummond lives here. Is she at home?' The door slammed shut in my face!

I stood there, listening. From the other houses in the row I could hear radios, a baby screaming its head off, a cistern being flushed. Across the road the two Pakistanis tried to start the rust-job. The battery had no life in it. One of them dived back under the body and the other's top half disappeared into the engine.

I knocked again. Feet came to the door.

'Go away,' came a woman's voice, deeper than the other one.

'Kathleen Drummond?' I said to the gaping letter box.

'Go away.'

'Sorry, I've got to see Nurse Drummond.'

The door opened and I found myself looking at the surprisingly fresh complexion and clear eyes of an erect, grey-haired woman wearing a fur coat, one hand holding the collar tight as if against a cold wind.

'There is no such person as Nurse Drummond,' she said severely.

'There used to be,' I said. 'I wonder if she'd like a chat about St Margaret's Hospital.'

'It's taken you long enough to come,' she said. 'Well then, are you coming in or not? I can't stand here getting my death of cold.'

Now that the thunderstorm had passed the sun was drying out the pavements. I could see the little wisps of vapour. But inside the low, dark house was like a steam-bath. I could hardly breathe, though whether that was from lack of oxygen or the stomach-turning odour I couldn't tell.

We climbed some frail stairs. Of the old woman with the eggshell skull there was no sign. She took me into a room off the landing.

I've been in worse rooms. Three of the four window panes were covered over by cardboard. Heavy curtains had been pulled back just enough to let in a faint glimmer of the sunshine through the fourth pane.

The room had two high-backed chairs, both occupied by neat piles of solidly compressed newspapers. Against one wall was a single bed. A small table was covered with an assortment of cups, jampots, school exercise books, biscuit tins seemingly full of newspaper cuttings, and a Leaning Pisa of thick books with tattered bindings.

She closed the door carefully.

'Do they know at St Margaret's that you've come to see me?' she asked. I put her accent down to East Anglia, Norwich maybe.

'Not exactly, perhaps I'd better explain. I work for this firm of solicitors, you see –'

'Yes, yes,' she said impatiently, 'I've been writing to your firm for two years. Was it them at the hospital who stopped you coming?'

'Oh, I see, you've been in touch with solicitors already?'

'That's a stupid question. Why would you be here otherwise?'

'Maybe you could tell me what you've been writing about.'

'You don't know?'

'Well, I'm new to the case so it would be better if you told me in your own words.'

'It's all in the books,' she said, pointing to the school jotters. 'What they did to me.'

'Can I have a look?'

'That's what they were written for. I wish them read out in the highest court in the land. The newspapers are frightened to print them – a very high editor told me they could not be printed until they had been read out before an eminent judge. You will know how to arrange that.'

I picked up the top exercise book.

'I could do with more light,' I said.

'Light?' She sounded resentful. 'I can see perfectly well.'

'Yeah, but my eyes are bad.'

'The switch is by the door.'

The room was a trifle more visible when I switched on one naked, low-wattage bulb hanging from the centre of the ceiling by a short flex. The first thing I noticed was that the bed was occupied by a large tabby cat nursing a young kitten. The light surprised the mother cat. She raised her head, front legs poised to spring from her hollow nest in the blanket. The kitten made tiny mews as it scrabbled to regain a hold of her teat. Kathleen Drummond stood by the table, looking at the window.

I didn't have to read much to know it was the old paranoia stuff, large capitals for key words, phrases underlined in different colours, frequent punctuation by five or six exclamation marks. The margins were scrawled over with additions and explanations.

She was a victim of a conspiracy by the administrators, doctors, consultants, matron, ward sisters, staff nurses and patients of St Margaret's Hospital.

Her efforts to obtain justice were being thwarted by the usual gang, newspaper editors, MPs, Catholic priests, television news-casters and the Archbishop of Canterbury.

She was a nut and nobody was ever going to get much mileage out of her in a witness box.

'What did they tell you at St Margaret's when they sacked you?' I asked.

'They did not sack me,' she snapped. 'They made me resign. They trick you by saying it's to safeguard your pension. It's their way of taking away your rights. They've had experience. Your superiors will understand.'

'Of course,' I said. 'But why did they tell you they wanted your resignation? I'll have to explain to my bosses when I get back to the office.'

'Lies and rubbish. They were all against me.'

'What kind of lies? We'll need the actual words to tell the court, you see.'

'They knew I was having to take medicinal relief for my back. They used that against me. The matron was jealous of me. She knew I had her measure.'

'You had a bad back?'

'They made me stand all day. I was in constant pain. They enjoyed that. Those women – they used to laugh at me and jeer behind my back.'

'What kind of medicine were you taking?'

'It was recommended to me by a colleague I thought I could trust but even she turned against me.'

'What was this stuff you were taking?'

Both Toni and Mrs Gunning had said she drank but I'd found that hard to believe. I've heard of senior consultants falling about like drunken sailors but the old pals' act doesn't usually cover the rank and file. Can you see the average ward sister letting her nurses roll back from the boozer with a good load on?

With Drummond it was different. I got part of the story from her and part from her weird writings.

As she grew older her back became more painful and some friend had put her on to the comfort of tonic wine, the stuff that generations of church-going spinsters, who would have called gnatpiss light ale the devil's brew, drank in the happy belief that the saints would have smiled.

It brought comfort and it wasn't sinful.

It was just alcoholic enough to get them hooked.

So that's how Drummond acquired the taste – and the need . . .

Although she regarded me as a mere messenger boy I managed to keep her talking. That's what I'm good at.

It has to be for I'm not much good at anything else.

'I think this will do for the summary of your case,' I said. 'Of course my superiors will explain it all in more detail but I can tell you one thing for sure – when you start this case they'll make up more lies about you.'

'I know the lengths they will go to.'

'Are you sure?'

She walked round the table, moving like a woman in pain but keeping a straight back and an implacable face. There was something almost ominous about the grim way she held onto her dignity. Mad or not, maybe it was only this weird obsession that held her together. I studied her face and tried to imagine what she would have looked like as a girl. What kind of life had it been for her? Had people always found her ugly – not just physically, there was a stony quality about her which I guessed she'd always had. Had she always been lonely?

There in that strange dark room I *felt* more about another human being than I have ever done, before or since. It wasn't exactly pity but that was part of it.

The eerie truth was, I felt as if I had known her all my life.

So it wasn't intuition that told me what to ask her next. I didn't even have to think about it. The words just *came*.

'You know they'll say you changed the babies over out of spite?' I said quietly.

For a moment the silence was hypnotic, like a bad dream. Her hands moved up and down the old fur coat. She stared down at the mother cat and the fat, squirming kitten.

'They'll never stop punishing me,' she said, slowly and deliberately.

She sat down on the edge of the bed and stroked the mother

cat's head. She made no sound but when next I looked at her face the tears were running down her cheeks . . .

I left that tiny, terraced house an hour later. I put her bundle of exercise books in the boot and locked it. I didn't look up at the cardboard window.

As I sat there, my hands on the wheel, the rain came on again. The two Pakistanis threw their tools into the oil-stained shopping bag and ran for the shelter of a door.

I started the car and reversed down Whitnell Street. There was one person I had to see. One lie I had to rub out.

Chapter Ten

The housing department had repaired the lift in Herbert Morrison House. I wished they hadn't. It was taking me up too quickly.

When Toni opened the door her face broke into a broad smile. She was wearing a white jumper with a deep v-neck and a short skirt.

I had told her I preferred skirts to trousers, on women. She had dressed this way to please me.

'Don't stare at me like that,' she giggled as we went into the living-room. The mock-log electric fire was on and the room was warm. The goldfish was nosing lazily against glass. It had grown accustomed to my face.

The mounted photograph of Patricia Abrey was no longer on the TV set.

'Coffee?' she said brightly.

'No thanks.'

'Yeah, let's forget the coffee, eh?'

She came towards me, arms raised to go round my neck. I moved back behind the orange settee, my fists clenched in the pockets of my suede jacket.

There was only one way I could go through with this.

She saw my expression and frowned.

'What is it?' she asked.

'You'd better sit. I've got something to tell you.' My voice was a flat monotone. I kept telling myself that thousands of kids were dying at this very moment, out there, somewhere. *Those* mothers had real troubles.

But my fists kept clenching tighter and tighter.

'Do stop play-acting, Jimmy,' she said.

'I said sit down.'

'Bossy, aren't we?'

I stood there on the other side of the orange settee until she was in one of the armchairs. My eyes never left hers. I didn't look once at her legs.

'Go on then, tell me the worst,' she said, forcing the cheeriness. 'Your Mummy's found out about us and says I'm not good enough for you.' I didn't smile. Her face fell. 'Didn't last long, did it?' she said bitterly.

'Maybe it should never have started,' I said. 'I'm here to tell you something you might find hard to believe but it's the truth. For starters I don't work in television, I don't have anything to do with television, I'm a private inquiry agent. I was sent here to do a report on you and Cliff and Tricia. I made up that yarn about television just to get into the house.'

She was frowning.

'I didn't know why they wanted a report on you,' I went on, voice without emotion. 'I was just told to trace a mother who'd had a baby in St Margaret's Hospital. You understand that? What happened with you and me had nothing to do with it.'

'Who told you to trace us?' she said, her head shaking slightly. I think she still thought it was a joke.

'A firm of solicitors in High Holborn, Venables, Venables, Williams and Gregory.'

'But why did you have to lie about it?'

'We were told to be discreet. Remember that appointment I was late for on Friday?'

She nodded. I took a few paces towards the window, my eyes never leaving hers. I could feel my nails biting into my palms.

'We met Georgina Gunning off the plane from Los Angeles. You remember her? In the maternity ward? She was the client who asked us to trace you.'

'Georgina? You mean she wanted to get in touch with us again? But we were never that pally – I mean, why go to all the bother – '

'You remember in the park, Saturday, Tricia's friend dropped her ice-cream and a woman gave her money for another one?'

'Yeah – but how do you know about *that*?' Her eyes were wide with astonishment.

'I was sitting on the grass on the other side of the lake. The woman who gave them the money was Georgina. We followed you there so that she could get a good look at Tricia.'

'At Tricia! Georgina did? And you followed – what the hell is this all about?'

'I'm going to tell you. I shouldn't be telling you anything but I'm going to. I don't want you to think I was deliberately doing the dirty on you. Just listen. The Gunnings had a car accident in California. Their kid needed blood transfusions. The doctors tested their blood groups and told them Helen couldn't be their child. She swears blind there's no other man could've been the father. So she decided there was only one explanation. Only two baby girls born that day – right? She thinks they were switched between delivery and bringing them into the ward for the first time. After that you'd have known you had the wrong kids.'

'Switched? The babies?'

'I'm telling you what *she* believes. You left the hospital with the wrong children.'

'No – it's a joke,' she said. 'Honest, Jimmy, you been drinking or anything? I – '

'It's no joke. How do I know about the park? You can find out for yourself if it's a joke. Phone Venables, Venables, Williams and Gregory and ask for Gregory. He'll tell you it's no joke. He'll sack me for having told you about it but at least you'll know I'm not lying.'

'But – *why*? What's she doing all this for?'

'She thinks she's going to take Tricia away from you and Cliff.'

'How the hell can she take Tricia away from us? What a load of old rubbish!'

But she wasn't so sure now.

'If she gets some kind of case together about the possibility of the kids being switched then she can go to court and ask for custody of Tricia. If the judge believes they were switched he might decide in her favour. If not she looks set to take it all the way to the House of Lords. She's got enough money. Personally I don't think she'll ever get near a court but you never know. That's why I came to tell you.'

'Very considerate of you, I'm sure.'

'If I'd known what it was all about from the start I'd – '

'You'd have what?'

She stared at me for a moment. Then she stood up, her face looking scornful.

'It's the biggest load of rubbish I've ever heard! Swapping babies over in a hospital? Who's ever going to believe that? The House of Lords? They ain't that daft. You must be a right berk to get mixed up in it, it's mad!'

'Yeah? You may be right. I'm only here to put you on your guard. It's no skin off my nose.'

'You're crazy, Jimmy. You think you're a hard case but you're silly, that's all. You and your bleeding knees. You're like a little boy who's never grown up, not your brains anyway.'

I knew it was a mistake but her sneer was too close to home. I allowed myself to get needled.

'Silly, is it?' I snapped. 'You should know. Who told me she'd never really felt like a proper mother? Eh? You said you didn't love Cliff and you often wondered why you didn't love Tricia as much as he does. You said she made you feel like a stranger. You said you'd just as soon meet somebody you could really love and just disappear with him and never see Cliff or Tricia again. You said you felt guilty about maybe being an unnatural mother because you didn't really love her, not the way mothers are supposed to. You said all that to me through there, in that bed. Just making conversation were you? Pillow talk was it?'

'You are a hard bastard,' she said, her face a deep red.

'Yeah, I know. Sorry.'

We stared at each other across the orange settee.

'So what happens next?' she said.

'Hard to say.'

'Is the general idea that we're supposed to get the other girl, in exchange? Like kids swapping footballers' autographs?'

'She hasn't thought that far ahead. I told you, I don't think it will ever get that far. But you had to know. I didn't want you finding out from anyone else.'

'Thanks,' she said, sarcastically. She chewed her bottom lip as she looked at me. Then her eyes narrowed.

'I suppose you think because I was easy to get into bed I'm a dope,' she said. 'Well, I'll tell you something, Jimmy, maybe I did say all those things about Cliff and Tricia. Maybe I was daydreaming about the kind of life I don't have here, not stuck in this flat, a dull little common housewife. But you let your rich friends know, if they showed me signed certificates from the Queen herself that Tricia wasn't my baby I wouldn't waste spit on them. Even if I ever believed all this codswallop, which I don't not in a million years, it wouldn't change what I feel about Tricia. Yeah, I know I'm always niggling at Cliff cos he goes on like an old woman but that's just the way most families go on. You wouldn't know that, not ever having had kids or a proper family of your own. Tricia's my baby and Cliff is my husband, for better or for worse. That's all I've got, isn't it? I don't *care* if there was a mistake at the rotten hospital, I don't even want to *know* about that other kid, Tricia is my little girl and Cliff is my husband and Georgina Gunning and your bigtime lawyers and all of you can go and boil your bloody heads.'

'That's okay then. I'm glad you feel that way.'

'That's nice for you. Now you'd better piss off, Jimmy, your time's precious, ain't it, five guineas an hour?'

'I'm not being paid for this.'

'Were you getting paid all those mornings last week?'

'You know that had nothing to do with it.'

'No? Wasn't you getting good information? I'll give you credit, you never actually said you loved me. I thought you were just being careful. I suppose you were making notes the whole time.'

'Think that if you bleeding like.'

'I think you're beneath contempt.'

'Sorry about that.'

I started towards the door. She followed me, her arms folded across her breasts.

'You can tell Georgina I feel sorry for her,' she said calmly. 'She brought up a kid for six years and now she's willing to give her away because of a few mouldy old blood tests? As a mother she must be a prize.'

'I won't be telling her anything,' I said, standing in the doorway. 'It's up to you what you tell Cliff.'

'I'll take care of that, don't worry about me, Jimmy,' she said. 'You aint the only hard one.'

We parted without a smile, her standing in the doorway with her arms folded, me taking the stairs rather than stand there waiting for the lift.

I got into the Stag and headed west.

My fingernails felt as if apprentice interrogators had been learning on them.

I still hadn't decided what to do about the conversation I'd had with Nurse Drummond by the time I got back to the mews in Kensington.

Maureen said my mother had phoned twice and was going to call back later in the afternoon.

'Was it important?' I asked.

'How should I know?' she snapped.

That's when I decided what I was going to do next. It was too easy to be a hard bastard. This town was full of sharp operators who left their emotions at home with their slippers.

Don't sneer. My heart was still the same old lump of leather. But I owed Toni *something*.

'I have to go out,' I said to Maureen. 'If my mother calls again tell her to ring me later tonight at Mancini's house. You've got the number, haven't you?'

'I think so, possibly.'

'Be warned – never come between a man and his mother.'

'That's the last – '

But I was going down the stairs.

It was just after five when I managed to find a parking space in Mayfair. I walked to Claridges. Luckily it was between showers. The water experts should have shown faith in the English summer. A few more days like this and we'd be exporting the stuff.

At the desk I asked them to try Mrs Gunning's room number but she was not there. I looked in the public rooms. I was hungry but high tea at Claridges isn't my speed.

I took a stroll into Oxford Street. It didn't seem such an ordeal without a wife trailing me from shop to shop. Droves of eager, anxious consumers flowed past the sex cinema. I can't remember what the attraction was that week, *My Swedish Meatball* maybe, or *Danish Dentist On The Job*.

It wasn't until I was dealing with a hamburger and a coffee in my usual manner, thirty bites to every chew, that I realized it was a whole two days since I'd had the horrors for a drink.

Did this mean I'd beaten it?

A lifetime of boring sobriety stretched endlessly ahead of me. I felt so depressed I forgot what the coffee tasted like and ordered another cup. A small Indian swept the floor round my feet. I watched him for ten maybe fifteen minutes. He never smiled or talked to anyone. He kept his eyes on the floor and his mind on some other, far distant place where he had a name.

I felt so depressed on his behalf I decided I needed a break from all this. A drive to Spain maybe, a few days on the Costa Blanca, the beaches knee-deep in frying typists from Birmingham, the cocktail bars full of jolly car-workers in paper hats, the soft Spanish nights redolent with the haunting scents of fish and chips. Terrific.

Back at Claridges they tried Mrs Gunning's suite again. No joy. I sat in the lounge and read the *Standard*. A loud cross-section of rich America trailed back and forth from the door to the desk.

I crossed my legs a lot. Nothing much was happening in the papers, a wages gang had got away with £89,000 in Pinner, London's new Labour bosses were planning radical moves but not now, an old widow had been raped and strangled in Camden Town, David Frost had a new girl, Battersea basements had been flooded by a cloudburst, new revelations were rocking the White House, the London football managers were again guaranteeing brighter soccer to bring back the missing millions, Centre Point was still empty, a teenager had been stabbed to death on his own doorstep, more old buildings were to come down to make way for more empty office blocks, London airport customs had pounced on cannabis worth £800,000 while London airport police were looking for a stolen consignment of diamonds worth £300,000. Oh yes, and our trade figures were the best for ten years. Or the worst, I can't remember.

Seeing it was dry again I went out and had a stroll round the interior of Mayfair. Wealthy middle-aged people brayed to each other in the entrances to restaurants that didn't have price menus outside. There's class for you. Uniformed chauffeurs relaxed with cigarettes in their masters' Rolls-Royces. A covey of bright young things in society gear whinnied on a balcony.

I knew they couldn't be real society. I mean, *nobody* hangs around dreary old London in August, Jeremy. They didn't even chuck plovers' eggs at me.

I walked round Grosvenor Square. The US Embassy was silent and huge and remote. I wondered if the eagle was bugged. I thought of Tricia Abrey and that fenced-off playground with the creaking swings and the lop-sided roundabout . . .

It was after seven when next I slid up to Claridges desk.

Yes, she was in and she would come down, if I cared to wait in the lounge?

Her face was hard, maybe just a little apprehensive, as she came towards me. She needn't have worried.

I was charm itself.

She was paying my wages, wasn't she?

The place I took her to in Soho was horrible.

I chose it carefully.

When we sat down I explained to Mrs Gunning that I often came here because I always felt uncomfortable in those snobs' restaurants. Here there was no fat, friendly proprietor who knew all his patrons by their first names, no smiling violinist relentlessly sawing Viennese crap at every couple, no elderly middle-European waiters full of nauseating clichés about love and life.

'You remember all the films?' I prattled, 'the hero always said to his society girlfriend, "they know me in a little Italian joint the tourists never visit". Momma came out of the back kitchen with a special plate of steaming wop-nosh – the hero's name was always Johnny – they put up the closed sign and had a party, gingham table cloths, an accordion, wine glasses raised in entwined arms. The society doll always said, "I really love your friends, Jahnny, they're so simple and happy and *genuine*". And the fat owner with the moustache had to wipe the tears away with the white napkin stuffed down his neck and he always said, "you musta come a backada areal soonada, Johnee, Momma'n me we tinka you asada son".'

She was looking at me doubtfully. I gave her a wink.

'It's not like that here,' I said, glaring round yet again to see if the staff's varicose veins would permit anything so energetic as bringing us the fiction they called a menu. 'The staff changes once a month. The boss lives in fear of the health department getting a look at the kitchens. Look at it, a little Italian place with an impersonality all of its own. Ask for spaghetti and you'll get just enough to lace your boots. What's the food like? Ask the boss – he eats across the road in the Wimpy bar.'

'What did you want to tell me?' she said, still looking at me doubtfully.

It was a good act. What did she have to worry about from a happy moron like me? A guy so clueless he got embarrassed in any restaurant where they hid the sauce bottle?

'I've been out for two days looking for this nurse – Drummond,' I said. 'I've also been digging up a few bits and pieces about the hospital. I think I may be onto something. Only it's a bit tricky.'

'How's that?'

The waitress brought us the menu. After we'd ordered I said we might as well smoke.

'It'll help to kill the next dreary hour. The thing is – well, Gordon wouldn't be too keen on my little idea.'

'Why not?'

'He's a bit of a nervous nellie. He wouldn't even like the idea of me seeing you alone like this. That's why I chose this dump, to be honest. Any decent place and there'd be just a chance we'd be seen. Suave London is a very small village.'

'Well, what is it?'

'I've met a lot of people who know Drummond. She was a lush all right. Or is – I've got a good lead to where she's living now.' I looked round suspiciously. 'You know she got the bullet from the hospital a week or so after you'd been in there? The thing is – why? That's why I had to see you on your own.'

'I don't really follow.' She sounded eager. I leaned forward.

'I'm taking a big chance on you,' I said. 'It's a cinch there's a file on her in the hospital records. They don't get shot of trained nurses without good reason. I'm betting that file would do your case a lot of good. Only – how do we get at it? Do it officially and you know what's likely to happen, don't you? The file just happens to be missing, aint that a shock?'

She looked at me. I nodded.

'That's it,' I said, holding up my right hand and rubbing my thumb and forefinger together.

She didn't just rise to the bait, she gulped it down.

'You mean you could break into the hospital and steal that file but Gordon Gregory wouldn't agree?' she said. I frowned for her to keep her voice down. 'Which means he wouldn't pay you. But you and I could come to some arrangement? How much?'

'I'd be sticking my neck out so far you could tie knots in it. If I'm tumbled I probably go down for eighteen months. The judges don't seem to like inquiry agents.'

'Name the price then.'

Our minestrone came at that point.

I waited until the grated cheese was going under for the third time.

'You really want to go that far?' I said.

'I told you, I don't care what it costs. If you knew what it meant to – never mind.'

'I'd want paying in advance,' I said, looking sly. 'In case I'm not here to take you out dining for a while.'

'Listen, the money is no problem. Any way you want it.'

'And Gordon?'

'What's he to me? Just a lawyer I was recommended to.'

'I was getting the idea you and him were – you know – just a little bit?'

'Oh for Christ sake.'

'And how would you tell him you'd got hold of the file?'

'You think of something.'

'I'll try – only I'm not too clever when it comes to telling the tale. Anyway, I'll start sussing out the hospital geography. But I won't actually make my move until I see if I can find that nurse – there's always a chance she'll cough and I won't have to risk a lagging.'

'You're bright enough,' she said.

From then on we were as thick as tea-leaves.

I suggested a bottle of wine. I said that watching her knock it back would remind me of better days.

Then I got down to the casual conversation.

'What's your husband think about all this?' I said through a mouthful of under-done steak. Under-done? The other end could still have been chewing grass.

'Oh Alan's like most men, he can't feel it the way I do, the way a mother would feel. He doesn't object to me being over here, if that's what you mean. He's always on to me about nipping over to London for a holiday.'

It struck me that she was speaking English now – the East End version. I took this as a compliment to my little turn. She trusted me and was willing to be her natural self.

The clever bitch!

'Got a family here?' I said.

'Just my mother but we don't get on. She's an old cow. Alan bought her a lovely bungalow at Broadstairs, she always liked Broadstairs but as soon as he'd paid over the money she decided it was too high up for her and too far away from her friends and too big to keep clean. Now she won't even go near the damn house. You got any family?'

'My wife and I split up. She left me for an architect twit, long-haired ponce. Thank Christ there were no kids. By the way, I'm sorry about that, the other day in Gordon's office. I didn't really think.'

'When I had my little emotional outburst?' She smiled. The wine bottle was past half-way. I topped up her glass. 'Don't worry about it.'

I waited but she went on slicing up her calves' kidneys.

'None of my business, of course but – '

'You mean what happens to Helen?'

'Cross that bridge when you come to it, eh?'

'That's about it.'

I poured her some more Italian white and rattled the plates to let the kitchen card-game know we were ready to risk the sweet.

I never used to like sweets but since I gave up boozing I found I liked my pudding, too true.

'It's a fascinating situation,' I said, with another of my casual openers.

'Fascinating? It's hell. But you think if you had any say in it you'd want to leave a kid of yours where the Abreys live? If you knew it was your child?'

'Oh no, I'd say you were coming on the scene like a fairy godmother.'

My teeth didn't turn black and fall out on the plate. I asked her if she'd like a brandy. Women don't have that male weakness of needing company to drink with. Otherwise why aren't the pubs full of guzzling housewives? She had two large brandies to my glass of French mineral water. I told a few jokes and waved my hands about like the happy little shyster I was.

It took two more brandies in that Soho place, another three large ones in the hotel bar and a lot of cheery nonsense from me before she really loosened up.

That's when I slipped it in.

No, not *that*.

The question. The point of my whole act.

'Yeah, breaking into the hospital won't be no problem,' I said, nudging her. 'I mean, they got no security, have they? What's a clever thief likely to want in a hospital, eh? Pickled kidneys in a green bottle? I'll get that file, don't worry. Then – bingo – you're as good as home. You get the kid.' Another nudge. 'In fact, you get both the kids, don't you?'

I grinned at her.

'We cross that bridge when we come to it,' she said. She tried not to smile. I leered villainously.

'You never did intend any swap, you sly old thing, did you? You can't kid old Jim-Jim. What – rescue one little girl from that dump and stick the other one back in its place? Course you're not. I sussed it out from the start. Good luck to you, too, I say.'

I laughed – at the permitted level for Claridges.

She'd had a lot to drink but she still knew a thing or two.

'That would be a pretty diabolical thing to do, wouldn't it?' she said.

'Why?' I looked particularly moronic. What did somebody say – a moral imbecile? I don't know about the moral.

'Wouldn't be fair, would it?' she asked.

'Fair? Oh well – look, I've only got one kiddie to look after – ' I tapped my chest – 'but it *was* on my mind a bit. Call me a silly, sentimental old fool but it would be a right liberty to give your kid the boot from sunny California into Herbert Morrison House. With Cliff Abrey for a new dad!'

I laughed.

'No, that won't happen,' she said quietly.

'Course it won't. I knew all along. How could you give up your Helen, you've loved her as your own for six years, haven't you? Try to get Tricia back by all means, sure, but nobody could be that hard – to do vice versa. Gordon should've given me the nod.'

I laughed again.

'You won't tell him I told you this? He said he was worried you'd gone soft on the Abreys. He said we shouldn't tell you because he thinks you've got an over-developed conscience.'

I said I could hardly believe it. I may even have sounded insulted.

'You want to have a nightcap in my suite?' she said. Her eyes were just a little bit hazy.

'No thanks, wish I could but I got a date with my mum.'

She laughed at that.

It was bucketing down outside. I threw my sopping jacket on the back seat and shot the Stag through Mayfair, out into Park Lane and then hot licks through Victoria and Chelsea. On that bottom stretch of the Kings Road I was doing over seventy.

So now I knew.

It had been a carve-up from the start. She wasn't going to

swap over the kids, she was going to get custody of Tricia and then leave the Abreys to stew. Even if they wanted to they didn't have the money to start any court cases in America to get custody of the other little girl. And even if a Sunday newspaper put up the lolly no American judge was ever going to send that child into poverty in a foreign country.

Gordon had known all along.

Hazell was just the legman who went out and told the lies. The rich, beautiful people had it all sewn up as usual.

Why was I driving like a lunatic? Because I was in a hurry. I was going to get back to Reggie's place and lock the door and get behind that big bar of his and drink myself stupid.

The whole thing was giving me headaches. Tomorrow I was going to chuck the whole thing in and ask Dot for that job in Birmingham. The hell with the money, I wasn't up to this kind of job.

They could all go to hell, Toni included.

Rain bouncing off my skull I ran for Reggie's front porch, right hand scrabbling in my pocket for my keys. I'd stay drunk for a fortnight and the whole thing would go away.

The phone was ringing when I got to the landing.

It was my mother.

'You've been out all evening,' she complained, the very first thing she said!

'I'm a big boy now,' I snapped.

'I've been trying to phone you all day – I was so worried about you.'

'What're you talking about – worried about me? You been drinking?'

'I'm all right, don't you worry. It's you that needs to worry. Keith O'Rourke and one of his mates was round our place last night. They wanted to know where you was living. We didn't tell 'em, mind, cos we didn't know. He said to tell you he's going to sort you out. I wanted to tell the police but your Dad wouldn't have none of that.'

'Jesus Christ! What did he do to you?'

'Don't worry about your Dad and me, son, he was trying to put the frighteners in but we was all right. We're staying at your Cousin Tel's place for a night or two, that was your Dad's idea. He says you got to look out for yourself, Jimmy.'

'Did he touch you?'

'Nah, he was trying to scare us but you know your Dad, take more than Keith O'blinking Rourke to make him lose his bottle.'

'I'll be over there in half an hour.'

'It's raining you know.'

There's a mother for you.

Chapter Eleven

My cousin Tel came down to the car with me. I stayed the night at his place in Hoxton, me and Mum and Dad. Tel wasn't really my cousin but my uncle. I called him Cousin because he was younger than me. He had a three-bedroomed flat in a high-rise. He and Sheree had three kids.

It was a crush but Dad said we hadn't had such a roisterous family night since the good old air-raid days in the shelter. I took his word for it.

Keith O'Rourke had tried to put in the frighteners but if anything he seemed to have taken ten years off the old man.

However, they promised to stay with Tel until I'd sorted out the O'Rourke situation.

It was ten past seven when I got into the Stag in the parking-space in front of the big block. It was going to be a sunny day. That was obvious, the sun was shining and the radio was forecasting rain.

'Don't go steamin' in on your tod, Jim-Jim,' Tel said, holding the car door. 'Them O'Rourkes niver goes in but mob-handed. You set it up an' give me the wire and I'll git a few of the chaps an' we'll rubbish the lot of 'em.'

'I'll let you know, Tel.'

'Be lucky.'

I drove to Putney. Early morning in London and you know what it must have been like before. Easy. Considering I was going to have to deal with a guy who wanted to give me stumps I was feeling good. I had to laugh at the old man, clever old bastard. He spent half the night telling me dead-cert ways of kicking Keith O'Rourke into touch. Putting a bomb in his car was about the most Christian.

This time I didn't roll the Stag into Reggie's driveway but

parked it in the next avenue and approached the house on the opposite pavement.

Before I let myself in I rang the bell and then slid round the corner of the porchway. Nobody answered. Whatever else he'd tried Keith hadn't found this address.

I needed a bath and a shave and a new shirt and something to eat but first of all I lobbed some grub into the fish tanks.

As far as I could tell the fire-mouth parents hadn't been wolfing down their nippers but I wasn't tending the fish out of any great interest in their welfare. It was tank number eight I paid most attention to.

That was where the paradise fish were, the worst killers of the lot, according to Reggie's instructions. On no account, said the label stuck to the front, were they to be put with other fish.

Rolling up my sleeve I shoved my arm in amongst these dangerous killers until my fingers were sinking into the high bank of gravel at the rear of the tank. I had to probe around a bit but eventually my fingertips touched something solid.

The house had been turned over quite a few times by Old Bill but it hadn't clicked about the gravel.

That was where Reggie kept his shooter.

Around nine, tidied up and smelling of Reggie's lemon and lime shaving soap I dialled the Scotland Yard number and asked for Detective Inspector Minty of the Flying Squad.

They said he hadn't turned up yet at the Big House. I left my number.

There was hardly any nosh left in the fridge. I had breakfast off a carton of yoghurt (strawberry flavour), the second half of a tin of peaches, and a lump of smoked cheese that hadn't actually turned to stone.

Then Minty rang.

'About what you said the other morning,' I said, 'I could be interested.'

'I thought you might be,' said the brutal Scotch voice. 'We'd better have a meet.'

'Yeah but I got to finish my baby caper first. Maybe Friday?'

'Aye. Give me a ring.'

'One thing you might help me – you know where Keith O'Rourke's hanging out?'

'Why?'

'Coupla points I've got to put him straight on. Personal.'

'We might be willing to give him a bit of a leaning on, for a friend.'

'Handsome of you. I just want to chat. You start on him I'll get a bad name. I know Keith, we were at the same school, he can be talked to.'

'Don't meet him in any lay-bys then. He's living with some brass Islington way. You want the number?'

He read it out.

'Thanks,' I said.

'I'll want more than your thanks.'

I brazenly parked the Stag in the white lines marked for senior partners and took the lift to the sixth floor of the big block in Holborn.

'Gordon free?' I said to creamy Diane.

'I'm not sure.'

'I'll save you the bother,' I said, pushing into his office.

I knew what I was going to say to him. I didn't get the chance.

As soon as he saw me he stood up.

'I didn't think I'd be able to get hold of you,' he said.

'Why, you want to dance?'

He patted his pockets and checked the stuff on his desk.

'No, don't sit down,' he said, 'we aren't staying.'

'Where are we going?'

'A quick bite in Chancery Lane and then we're off to Bethnal Green, James. I've been discussing this affair with my father. He's still got it up here, I grudgingly have to admit. All set?'

'What's in Bethnal Green?'

'You're going to introduce me to Mr and Mrs Abrey, James. No more hole in the corner stuff.'

'Abrey won't be there, he's on a picket line.'

'No, the strike's collapsed. I've been rather busy this morning. You were right, I spend too much time looking down from a high window. Quite invigorating, a little bit of sleuthing. I decided we had to see him so I phoned his place of work to leave a message. The firm went bust last night, the management gave the communist-inspired strikers their cards and told them to try picketing the Kremlin. Jolly good, eh? They're blaming it on unfair Common Market competition but I don't see many of these small outfits surviving, do you? Best thing that could happen.'

'So they don't know we're coming?'

'I don't think one needs an appointment at that social level, does one?'

As we passed Diane's desk he told her he would be back around four.

As we went down in the lift I tried to remember what I'd gone there to tell him in the first place. Oh yeah – that was it. I was going to slide out from this job and go to work for Dot in Birmingham, as a wages clerk. At a tenner a day?

Forget it, I told myself. You aren't a coward, are you?

No, but I was smoking heavily as we took the firm's Mercedes into the exotic East End. Cliff Abrey was going to enjoy all this good news, wasn't he?

It was five to two when I gave the Abrey bell-button the lightest thumb since Tom went on a diet. Maybe they'd gone out, I thought, Gordon looming busily behind me. Maybe they were watching an afternoon soap opera and would think my dainty buzz was only an improvement in the dialogue. Maybe – '

The door opened.

I tried to smile politely. Toni's face was colder than an Eskimo's nose in a freeze-up.

'Mrs Abrey, I'm James Hazell – I called on you a couple of weeks ago,' I said quickly. 'This is Gordon Gregory, he's a solicitor, we'd like a word with you and your husband, if that's possible.'

Her eyes could have been charged with conspiracy to murder. I could only hope she realized she had more to lose than I did . . .

Gordon had explained it over a low-calorie, high-salary lunch. His father said this was not a criminal case and there had to be a genuine attempt to settle it amicably. But if it did reach court the firm must not in any circumstances look as if it had been furtively conspiring to rob a humble English mother of her only child.

'But shouldn't we hold fire till I've sussed out the hospital scene?' I asked. 'I'm right behind that old nurse.'

'Good,' he said, 'but from here on the Abreys have to be in the picture. Proving that a mistake was made is only part of it. The real battle will be to get custody for Mrs Gunning and every move we make has to be judged on how it will look in court. Anyway, who knows, they might be as anxious as our client to restore these children to their rightful homes. Abrey being redundant could be a big help to us.'

'Yeah?'

'It might make him more amenable to some form of arrangement. It would hardly make him more desirable a person to have custody in the eyes of the court, would it?'

'Dole queue versus millionaire's mansion, you mean?'

His knife sliced exquisitely into a piece of underdone rump steak that was costing more than a gruel banquet for the whole orphanage. He took a sip of the '63 and belched delicately behind a fine hand.

'I shouldn't let the human considerations upset your emotional balance, James,' he drawled. 'For five guineas an hour it's hardly your responsibility is it?'

They teach them that at Eton, how to slap down the servant class without use of strong language.

I let myself be slapped down.

I was pig in the middle but what could I do? Squeal?

I just had to face up to it. I was a hard case in a hard world and that was the only reason people paid me to stay alive . . .

'Oh yeah, about the telly programme is it?' Cliff said with a sad little smile. He got up from the formica-topped table in the kitchenette. For a moment I was puzzled by the coloured tissue paper and scissors he'd been using. Then I realized he was cutting out paper-hats.

Tomorrow was Tricia's birthday. August the sixth.

Poor Cliff, I thought.

He hadn't been Laugh a Minute Larry before but now he looked like a burst balloon.

It didn't take him more than thirty seconds to size up Gordon as a toff. I could have hit him, he was so subservient and apologetic.

I waited until we were in the living-room.

'The goldfish died this morning,' he said, seeing me look at the TV set. 'You must have been right about the feeding. Been our day, hasn't it, Toni?'

She stood with her arms folded and stared at me.

Gordon had his head bent forward although there were several spare inches between his skull and the ceiling. You have to be conditioned from birth for rooms this size.

'I'd better tell you straight away,' I said, standing at the opposite end of the orange settee. 'I'm not from television, Mr Abrey, I'm an inquiry agent and I work for Mr Gregory's firm.' Cliff frowned but I went on talking, trying hard not to catch Toni's eye. 'I told you a lie about the TV show because I didn't want you to know what I really was. I'm sorry about that.'

Gordon coughed. Cliff was confused but he pointed Gordon in the direction of an easy chair. It was so low Gordon's knees were level with his chest. He tried to look dignified. Toni went on standing there.

'Mr Hazell was working on my instructions,' he said. 'I apologize for the deception but at the time we had no idea why our client wanted information about you and we had been asked to be discreet.'

'Oh yeah?' said Toni. 'Anybody can just walk in off the street and you'll start snooping as long as they can fork up the cash?'

'It's not just as easy as that.' Gordon smiled patronizingly. Nobody else did. 'Normally we'd require satisfactory answers to the obvious questions but in this case our instructions came from abroad – America to be precise, a reputable legal firm we often deal with. It was only a routine tracing inquiry as far as we knew – then.'

I risked a look up at Toni. Her eyes were mocking me, in a savage sort of way. Cliff moved uncomfortably in the other orange chair. Toni's manner was disturbing him and he kept giving me baffled looks.

I was thinking that being done over by Keith O'Rourke would be fun compared to this.

'It's going to come as a bit of a shock to you both,' Gordon said sympathetically, 'I think the best thing is for me to outline the facts as I know them to date. You had your baby in St Margaret's Hospital, Mrs Abrey, August the 6th, nineteen –'

'I know when I had my baby,' she snapped.

'Of course. There was another woman in the ward who had a baby girl on the same day, a Mrs Georgina Gunning.'

'Yeah – Georgina,' said Cliff, apparently happy at recognizing *something* that we weren't keeping secret from him.

'Six or seven weeks ago Mrs Gunning and her husband were involved in a car accident in California,' Gordon went on. 'Their little girl – Helen – needed an urgent blood transfusion. I won't bother you with the details but the blood tests seemed to indicate that Mr and Mrs Gunning could not be the child's parents – not both of them at any rate. Mrs Gunning now believes that a mistake was made at the hospital.'

'A mistake?' said Cliff.

He was the only one in that room who didn't know. I suppose I did feel sorry for him, in a lazy kind of way. I wasn't even too bothered if Toni did blurt out something that told them I'd been seeing her on the sly.

What was the worst that could happen to *me*?

That's right. Birmingham, as an undercover wages clerk at ten quid a day.

'That's what she believes,' said Gordon. Everything about him, his suit, his accent, his very fingernails, seemed totally wrong for that room. It's what keeps the class system going, isn't it, the fact that the classes never see into each other's houses? One hour of forcing the Gregorys of this country to live like the Abreys and we'd have the biggest wave of progress since children were rescued from the coal-mines.

I mention these deep thoughts just to prove how cool I was keeping.

'A mistake – about the babies?' Cliff stammered. He looked up at Toni but her face was showing nothing.

'She thinks you got the wrong children, to put it simply,' said Gordon. He made a sympathetic little grimace. 'This is going to be hard for you to assimilate, out of the blue like this, I know that, Mr Abrey – and Mrs Abrey – '

'You mean, she thinks we've got her – our Trish is her baby?' said Cliff slowly. 'And her kid is really ours? Is that it?'

'I'm afraid so,' said Gordon. 'However, there's a long way to go.'

'A long way to where exactly?' Toni's voice was like the invitation to a beheading.

'This visit is as embarrassing to me as it must be to you,' said Gordon, 'but I felt in all the circumstances you had to know that the situation exists and – '

'What situation?' said Cliff, leaning forward a little.

'The situation as it affects you and the Gunnings,' said Gordon. 'What we have to do now is start thinking about the future of these children.'

'What future, how do you mean?' asked Cliff. He seemed to be steadying himself. I gave Toni another look. She glared at me as though she had just thought of something else.

I couldn't imagine what. Was there anything worse?

'The position is that Mrs Gunning has instructed us to take all possible steps to have her child – your Patricia – restored to her,' said Gordon.

'She has, has she?' said Cliff. 'She can take steps, can she? What steps exactly?'

'There is a great deal of legal precedent,' said Gordon. 'I sincerely hope it doesn't come to this but in the last resort she can claim care and custody of the child in court. What the judge decides, of course – '

'Legal precedent?' Cliff said slowly. 'Court? Judge? You mean she can do all that? Just because she thinks – '

'Look, Mr Abrey, I realize how this must sound to you, coming so unexpectedly, and believe me, I have no wish to get us all involved in a public fight, but I wouldn't have come here if I hadn't been reasonably convinced that Mrs Gunning has a case. What we have to do is – '

'What we have to do?' said Cliff. 'What case has she got? All she knows is some rubbish about blood groups – '

'There is more to it than that,' Gordon said, without so much of the honey.

'You dirty bastard,' Toni said quietly. We all looked up at her. She was staring at me.

'Mr Hazell was only doing what I instructed him to do,' said Gordon.

'You shit,' she said. 'You rotten, lying shit.'

'It aint Mr Hazell's doing, Toni,' said Cliff firmly. 'He's only the snooper.'

'Aint it? Ask him about Nurse Drummond then! I know where they're getting their bleeding case! And I bloody well helped you!'

I looked Cliff Abrey right in the eye.

'You remember I asked you both to try and remember anything more about the hospital?' I said. 'At the time it was just part of the – of the lie I was telling you. Your wife happened to see that old nurse in the street and gave me a ring.'

'Yeah and now they're going to use her, say she was drunk and put the babies in the wrong cots,' Toni shouted. 'They'll get her into court, they'll pay her to say she done it!'

'You never told me about that, Toni,' Cliff said quietly.

It was a nice moment while it lasted.

It lasted longer than the Ice Age.

'We won't be paying anybody to say anything,' Gordon said brisky. 'What I want to propose to you now is that – '

'What *you* want to propose?' said Cliff, slowly getting to his feet.

'We must try and see what kind of arrangement is possible, a situation – '

'There aint no situation as far as I'm concerned,' said Cliff, walking to the door.

'I don't think you quite understand, Mr Abrey, this unhappy state of affairs – '

'I'm happy,' said Cliff, opening the door.

Gordon didn't even blink.

'My client can start legal proceedings or we can discuss this in a civilized manner,' Gordon said. 'I should advise you that Mrs Gunning is extremely wealthy. The child's future is the main consideration and a suitable arrangement might be possible whereby – '

'She'd slip us a good whack, would she?' said Cliff.

I would have sworn he could see a joke.

'Do you have a solicitor?' Gordon asked.

'No but I do have a fucking good idea,' said Cliff, 'you and your snooper here, out!'

Gordon shrugged. We both stood up.

'I shall be writing to you,' Gordon said, nodding courteously at Toni. 'In the meantime I strongly advise you to get in touch with a good solicitor. Perhaps when you've had time to – '

'Out!' snapped Cliff.

Gordon did not exactly ignore him but he showed no sign of panic.

'I know how you must be feeling – ' he began.

'I'll give you one minute,' Cliff said quietly, 'If you aint at the top of the stairs you'll be at the bottom.'

He stood back to let us out. Just for a moment I was behind Gordon.

'It'll be all right,' I whispered to Toni, so quietly it was more like lip-language.

She took a step nearer me and spat in my face.

'Either of you two berks come near this house again with your fairytales I'll shove your faces down your bloody throats,' said Cliff.

He closed the door without slamming it.

I waited until we were going down.

'You think he wants to make it difficult for you?' I asked Gordon.

He was peering closely at the stuff written on the grey paint of the lift walls.

I touched my eyes and nose with my fingertips until I felt them wet. I dried myself with the back of my hand.

'I didn't expect any other reaction,' he said, almost absent-mindedly. 'Did you? Listen to this gem – my sister has terrific bristols and I want to strip her off! I must say! These places are even bleaker than they look on television.' He turned his face from the wall and looked at me. We seemed very close. I hoped my face was dry. 'You didn't tell me she was actively assisting in your enquiries, James,' he said.

'She thought it was for my television programme.'

His eyes stayed on my face.

'One would have expected her to make the fuss. You said she was the dominant partner. Yet I got the impression she wasn't even surprised. I wonder why.'

'Maybe she gets premonitions.'

'I wonder.'

In the end my eye was steadier than his and he looked at the wall.

'So what happens now?' I said.

'We report to Mrs Gunning and tell her the general reaction is antipathetic. Then we start the ball rolling.'

She kept quiet all the time. Then she spat in my face. Close-up, her eyes glaring, her lips making a circle. Right in my eyes.

No other word for it. I was *shocked*.

We crossed Sutherland Avenue to where the firm's uniformed chauffeur was sitting in the Mercedes. In that street it was as inconspicuous as an armoured troop-carrier in the Bogside.

I huddled into a corner and waited for Gordon to give the driver the word. When I looked round he was staring at me.

'Well?' he said.

'Well what?'

'She told you where the nurse is to be found, didn't she?'

I looked out of the window on my side. Across the road there were three boys, one tall, two short, one black, two white, all three thin-faced and sharp-eyed.

'Sit here much longer and we'll be selling tickets,' I said. 'Doesn't take long for the system to brainwash them, does it? They already respect what they'll never get.'

'I don't suppose you think I could survive among all this, James,' said Gordon softly.

'You should know.'

'Yes, I know how hopelessly effete I must seem in this context. But it's only protective colouring, James, camouflage. I'm not in my normal environment, that's all. I wouldn't underestimate me.'

'What's that supposed to mean?'

'I wouldn't like to think you were making a mistake.'

'Such as?'

'With my help you have a future, James, a much better future than you would have expected a few months ago.'

'Thanks.'

'I hope you're being careful, James.'

'If I can't be careful I'll be good.'

'Be flippant if you must. But be careful.'

'Meaning?'

'Meaning I hope you remember which side you are on.'

'I'm not that important.'

'We all have our various functions. If I have to be crude – I'd make an extremely unpleasant enemy, James.'

I knew what was coming and I made up my mind as I watched a woman with a pram stop beside the three boys to see why they were staring across the street at the big black Merc.

'Yeah,' I said, looking out of the window, 'she did tell me where that old nurse lives.'

I felt him moving on the seat. The driver just sat behind the wheel, staring ahead, ear cocked for his master's voice.

'Funnily enough I knew you were holding out on me back up there in that execrable little living-room,' he said. He didn't sound angry. He had the voice of a patient schoolteacher. 'Mrs Abrey glared at you the whole time. I would have expected her to make the fuss and I would have expected it to be directed at me – as the villain of the piece. But she stared at you and didn't even seem surprised at what I was telling them. She just stared at you. What exactly did you promise her, James?'

'Nothing.'

'Do you feel sorry for them?'

'Not sorry, no.' I turned my head towards him. 'But that kid is all they've got.'

'In ten or twenty years she will drop on her knees and give a prayer of thanks to us for taking her out of that slum over there. And it wouldn't be simply a case of taking away their child, Mrs Gunning has a little girl as well, you know, if we –'

'And she intends to keep it, doesn't she? Both kids, that's what she wants. You know the Abreys will never have the dough to go to law in America – even if they wanted to swap for some American brat they've never seen, which they don't. You've known all along? Georgina gets both kids and that pair of schmucks up there get left with a few snaps and some memories to cry over?'

'Not exactly. Some kind of arrangement can be reached – shared holidays, trips – money won't be any difficulty, we could even –'

'Yeah, money,' I said. 'Doesn't it ever worry you, that you only help people who have money? No matter the rights and wrongs?'

He didn't know it but I was giving him his last chance. I was tired of being patronized.

'Without money there are only wrongs,' he said. 'Would you rather be sitting in a Mercedes earning five guineas an hour – and bonuses – or back working behind a bar counter?'

I was wrong. He was giving me my last chance. It wouldn't take more than a hint dropped here, a raised eyebrow there. The word would be out that James Hazell was unreliable. The other big legal firms would get the message by lunchtime tomorrow. I had used up my ration of careers. It was this or Birmingham.

'And bonuses, you said?' I heard myself saying.

As we drove away from Herbert Morrison House I looked up at the eggbox windows.

It's a hard world and your only duty is to number one, I told myself.

My hand kept wandering up to feel my face.

Chapter Twelve

As I grunted directions to Gordon's driver I was still trying to convince myself this wouldn't be the end of it for Cliff and Toni.

Kathleen Drummond was nobody's idea of a good witness. The Abreys would get legal aid. The state would fix them up with a good mouthpiece. The papers would be on their side.

'By all accounts she's a bit addled in the brainbox,' I said as the Mercedes moored grandly against the broken pavement of Whitnell Street.

'Take it very easy,' he said. 'This whole affair could become pretty hairy. If the press got to hear of it prematurely we could be made to look extremely unpopular. All of us.'

The sun was shining and across the road the two Pakistanis were still working on their car. At least there were two pairs of feet sticking out from under it.

I led Gordon to the mangy door. I gave the woodwork as much stick as my knuckles would allow.

What the hell, I was thinking, I don't care, do I? Maybe the bleeding child would be better off in California. Who was I to decide its future?

There was no movement inside the house. I stood back and looked up at the window with the cardboard panes.

All four panes, glass and cardboard, had been smashed in.

'Was you lookin' for Mrs Delve?' said a woman's voice.

It came from the upstairs window of the next house but one. I got a glimpse of a head and then the window banged shut.

Gordon and I looked at each other. Then a door opened and she came out onto the pavement.

'Only they've tyken 'er away this mornin', unthey?' she said. 'In a ambulance, the welfare done it orl.'

She had frizzy hair, ginger, to go with her freckles. She was in her early twenties, as good-looking a red-haired spade as I've seen. Her kitchen must have been very hot for she wasn't wearing much, just a sleeveless, backless blouse and a thin, tight skirt.

Gordon spoke to her as if she was foreign, slowly, exaggerating the movements of his lips.

'We're actually looking for –'

'What's happened then, love?' I said, moving between them.

'Aint you from the council? Cos if you are I fink it's a bleedin' shame, that poor old woman an' nobody takin' a blind bitta notice. Disgustin' I say.'

'No, we're not from the welfare,' I said. 'Where's the one that was lodging upstairs?'

'Wot, ol' Smelly Drawers?'

'Kathleen Drummond, you mean?'

'I dunno wot her name was, do I? The kids call her Smelly Drawers. You won't get her, she done hersel' in, dint she? Gas, wunnit? Didn't surprise me none neither. She was 'orrible, made Mrs Delve's life a bleedin' misery she did. Best thing she ever done, wunnit, gas herself like? You from the insurance are yer?'

'You say Kathleen Drummond killed herself?' said Gordon. I don't suppose his type realize they are speaking loudly. I half expected every occupied house in the street to throw open its door and a large crowd to gather.

Across the road the two Pakistanis were practising diving starts into the engine of their old piece of salvage.

She told us the whole story, that good-looking freckled redhead with the flat nose. Drummond had filled the gas meter with shillings and turned on the gas ring. In the middle of the night Mrs Delve had heard the cat screaming but she was too infirm to climb the stairs so she had tottered out into the street, that old woman with the eggshell skull, and scratched on the red-head's window and they'd found Drummond's door barred from the inside and somebody had run two or three streets to the nearest phone box, which was just between one vandalization and the next, and the police, fire and ambulance had whooped into Whitnell Street and there hadn't been such a night of drama and community spirit since the Luftwaffe.

Drummond was dead and the welfare had dragged old Mrs Delve off for care and protection.

Turning out lucky for everybody, wasn't it?

So I thought.

As we sat in the back of the Mercedes heading back to the west and civilization I was careful not to sound cheerful.

But I was thanking the Gas Board prematurely.

'At least that simplifies matters,' said Gordon.

'I should cocoa.'

'Yes, we can pin the whole thing on the nurse without the inconvenience of presenting her in court. It's an old lawyers' maxim that I'm just inventing; dead witnesses never contradict themselves.'

'You got enough of a case?'

'I'm sending the file over to one of our most distinguished QCs this afternoon. We'll probably have to start by getting a court order to submit the Abreys for blood grouping. I must read up on blood groups, I think there's more to it. We may even decide to have Tricia Abrey made a ward of court. Just in case they're tempted to flee the country with her.'

'I don't think they've even got passports,' I said.

'I was joking, James.'

That's how deeply it was affecting us smart people.

The hell with it, I thought, it's out of my hands. I had business of my own to attend to.

I made the call from my cubby-hole in Dot's office.

A woman answered with a suspicious, 'Yeah?'

'I got a message for Keith,' I said, in my normal voice. 'I hear he's looking for James Hazell.'

'Just a – '

'No, you listen, darling. Just tell him a friend of Mr Minty's rang to say that Hazell's living in Reggie Mancini's house in Putney, the address is in the book. You got that, love? Reggie Mancini's house in Putney.'

'Keef's 'ere, I'll – '

I put down the phone.

I stared at the map, tracing the route from Islington to Putney. Knowing Keith he would start off being cautious and then say the hell with it and come steaming in, mob-handed.

I'd be waiting.

I was a hard man. Yet my hand kept rubbing over my face. Her lips pressed together, her eyes were glaring – and warm spit was slapping on to my cheek.

She'd said she lóved me and I'd immediately gone all itchy, sensing a trap. But I hadn't been able just to slide out.

Love, was that the word?

It's not a word I use too often. All I knew was that I couldn't remember any other week in my whole life when I'd felt so good.

No, better than that. I'd felt like a king. As if all the dreams had come true. Like you were supposed to feel, in the story-books.

And I didn't even know, not until it was over. Not until she spat in my face.

I could have cried for my own stupidity.

Instead I went downstairs to see Dot and told her most of it.

At the end she poured herself another brandy, looked me full on and rasped:

'If I'd been her I'd have gouged your eyes out while I was at it.'

'Yeah, okay, but what can I do? It's all sewn-up. You know something, the Abreys can't win, no matter how the case goes. It'll tear that family apart, the court case, it'll be like a Roman circus.'

She sat there for at least two minutes, silently staring at the glass in her hand.

'I hate the very sound of that Gunning woman,' she said at last. 'What kind of mother is she going to be?'

'Does that matter? I'm only interested in trying to do something for Toni, the rest is just –'

'Yeah yeah, you've screwed her a few times and now you're all guilty. Bullies or little boys, no in-between, that's what I think of men.'

'I don't need any bloody lectures – '

'Just a minute,' she said, putting down the glass. She sounded excited. She swivelled her chair round and starting digging into a shelf of untidy books and papers. Then she found what she was looking for, a red address book with ballpoint scribbles all over the covers. She threw it across the desk.

'Look up Los Angeles,' she said, 'I can't remember the name.'

'What name?'

'The name of the firm I've got down there to be used if we have any enquiries in Los Angeles.'

'You think I should write and ask them for a job?'

'Look, brainless, what do you actually know about this Gunning woman? Give these people a ring and ask them to do a bit of quick checking. Say you're working for me. You'll get a bill later.'

'What can he find out? We know all we need to know about her, she's rich, her husband is – '

'You know what she's told you, that's all. Call yourself an inquiry agent and you don't even follow the golden rule – check and double-check?'

'She wouldn't be daft enough to – '

'Check it anyway. Go on, it's worth a spit in the face, isn't it?'

I wrote down the number of Jonathon Bowles Investigations and went back upstairs. I gave the international operator the number and sat back to wait. It wouldn't do any good but at least I could say I'd tried.

Who could I say it to? Apart from myself. And I didn't put a lot of faith in anything I said anyway. Four mornings, that's all it was. Passed by like a flash. One short week.

The only truly happy week of my whole life and I didn't even know I was having it.

I saw her eyes glaring and her lips screwing up and the tendons standing out on her neck. Right in my face.

It had taken that to tell me.

Love? Yeah, that was the word. I couldn't think of any other for what was making me want to weep my stupid heart out.

The call came through in seven minutes.

Jonathon Bowles was having a good time, whatever time that was over there, across the ocean and the continent.

'Mr Bowles, this is the Dorothy Wilmington agency in London, England,' I shouted.

'How's that again?' came the American voice.

I heard him shouting to somebody to can the noise. I even heard the other person shouting back. When he understood who was calling I explained what I wanted.

'Gunning,' I said, 'G-U-N-N – yes, N for Nixon – you know, N-I-X-O-N – your president. That's it, Gunning. His first name is Alan. That's right, one L. He's in the music business, a record company. No, I don't know the company's name but he's a big wheel – no, not heel, wheel. Important! Yes, that's it, a big wheel. So what I'd like is some dope on the family – they had a car accident a few weeks back – yes I know there are a million people in the music industry, Mr Bowles, you want the titles of some of the hit records he's produced? . . .'

In the end he said he would make a coupla phone calls. He promised to ring me back, person to person. I gave him Reggie's number and Dot's number. I heard his girlfriend shouting impatiently in the background. Maybe it was his wife. The whole thing was stupid. I didn't even know I loved her until she spat in my face. Wasn't that typical of the whole mess I'd made of my life?

Then I remembered Keith O'Rourke and I got out of Dot's office and got in the Stag and drove to Putney in the middle of the rush-hour traffic. The sun was still blazing and the windows of the cars were rolled down, shirt-sleeved men sitting with their elbows poking out, car radios rising and falling as the lines edged over the bridge.

None of them looked happy.

I drove the car slowly past Reggie's house. I was wearing the sunglasses. I couldn't see any signs but there wouldn't have been any signs anyway. I parked the car in the other avenue.

Again the bell rang in an empty house. I opened the door, scraped my feet on the floor of the hall and then tip-toed back out onto the porch before I slammed it shut.

I listened but I heard nothing.

It was too far out of his home ground for Keith to be operating in broad daylight but I took no chances. I went round to the rear of the house and checked the downstairs windows.

There was a new extension at the back, running out of the kitchen. I pulled an empty wheelbarrow against the end wall of the extension and climbed up onto the flat roof.

When I looked in the first floor window of the big lounge I could hardly see for brilliant sunshine pouring in through the windows at the other end of the room.

The whole thing was stupid.

I dropped down from the extension and walked round to the front and let myself in and climbed the stairs.

Nobody jumped me.

The house was empty.

I made sure all the windows were bolted and checked the chains and locks on the back door. The front door I left on the latch so that it could be opened with a push.

I went to tank number eight and fished down into the gravel and came up with the oilskin package. It was a Luger automatic, black, rectangular, cold to the touch. It was loaded. I stuck it into my trouser waist and went down to the kitchen and ate the last two cartons of yoghurt and drank two pints of milk and went upstairs and sat in the lounge and waited.

Chapter Thirteen

It was a long night. Nothing much happened. I watched all the TV programmes, right to the very end. Just after midnight they had a pulsating interview with a guy who ran a public lavatory. It was a series about dull jobs. The old geezer said the job made him feel clean. I wondered how many millions had stayed up to catch the show.

Nobody came hammering on the front door or crashing through the downstairs windows.

There were a couple of phone calls, one was from a female supervisor at the telephone exchange. She said there was a fault on the lines and could I tell her what number I was speaking from.

She was very chatty.

She kept me talking for some time. Said it was boring at nights. Then we rang off.

I dialled the exchange and asked for the supervisor.

No, there were no faults on the lines. And the night supervisor was a man.

That was Keith all right, trying to be clever. He would have been listening on an extension. He would know if it was me from the voice.

The point was, would he come barging across London there and then? I thought not. He would want to suss out the geography, check if I was on my own. I went downstairs and locked the front door.

Never mind, I went to bed with the Luger in my right hand. Clever or not, Keith was still a nutter. A geezer who would cripple or kill because of a chip on his shoulder wasn't to be reckoned by logic.

I went to sleep straight away.

Funny, that. When I'd nothing to worry about I was always too tense to drop off.

Something woke me far on into the night.

I came out of my sleep faster than a team of dips scattering with a lifted wallet. The Luger was still in my right hand. I tiptoed across the rugs and stood sideways in the shadows by the door, looking across the landing and down the stairs.

It was the phone!

Jonathon Bowles was calling James Hazell, person to person, Los Angeles to London.

I held it against my chest for a second, listening. There was no other sound from the rest of the house.

'I located this guy Gunning,' Jonathon Bowles boomed across space. 'Can you hear me okay?'

I don't know what time it was over there but Jonathon Bowles was still at it, music and a woman's loud voice. I could hear him as plain as if he was standing beside me but he couldn't hear himself. He repeated everything he said as though it was written down in front of him in a foreign language.

But I got it all, in the end.

I didn't know Jonathan Bowles's secret, for he sounded like a guy who lived at some pace, but he knew his job all right.

It was more than I could have hoped for. Toni would want to kiss my face clean of the memory of that spit.

I repeated the phone number he gave me. It was dark and I couldn't remember where there was a pen but I've always been good at remembering phone numbers.

'That's great,' I said, 'I can't thank you enough, Mr Bowles.'

In the background at his end I heard the female voice shouting at him.

'You're welcome any time,' he said hurriedly, 'I'll mail you my itemized bill.'

He was already snarling at the female in the background as he put down the phone.

I felt my way round the end of Reggie's cocktail bar and opened the little fridge. The Luger was black and square and ugly in the light that flooded down on the wire shelves. I put it down beside the gleaming bottles and unscrewed the cap of a tonic water and gave my sticky mouth a cold, bitter sluicing. Then I went back to bed.

So that was that.

I should have dropped off a much-relieved man but I didn't. Each time I started to picture the scene where Toni came towards me with her arms raised to go round my neck I kept seeing the lonely figure of Georgina Gunning walking round the lake in Valentine's Park.

She must have been mad to think she could get away with it.

Mad?

Or desperate?

I could not get to sleep. Not a bloody wink.

I was the last man alive who should have been landed with the responsibility of deciding what was best for a six-year-old girl in Bethnal Green.

The arrival of Keith O'Rourke with a sawn-off shotgun would have been a blessed relief but he didn't show.

I knew he would come. That trick phone call from the woman pretending to be the exchange supervisor proved he was already making his plans.

If I hadn't had my Mum and Dad to think of I would have washed and shaved and packed my gear and asked Dot to direct me to Birmingham and never come back to London again.

I was on Toni's side, wasn't I?

So why did I keep on saying to myself, Poor Georgina?

Why the hell did women ever start having babies anyway?

I gave Georgina every chance.

I phoned her at Claridges, first thing in the morning.

'When are you going to get that file from the hospital?' she said, instead of good morning.

'That's off,' I said, 'look, Mrs Gunning, I – '

'Why is it off? You trying to raise the ante? For Christ's sake, name the price.'

'It's got nothing to do with money – '

'Well, what the hell has it got to do with? Was Gordon Gregory right, you're on their side?'

I couldn't just blurt it out, could I? Knowing what I knew about her? What Jonathon Bowles had found out?

'Mrs Gunning,' I said, licking my lips, 'don't you think it would be best for everybody if you just forgot this whole idea and went quietly back to –'

'No!'

She put down the phone on me. I rang Claridges again but she wouldn't speak to me.

I then rang Gordon's number at home.

The thin-boned wife answered.

'Speak to him at the office,' she snapped.

'I want to bloody speak to him now,' I snarled.

'You disgusting little man,' she said. She put down the phone on me as well.

What the hell did she mean, *little*? I'm almost six feet tall.

I left Reggie's house by the back door but there was nobody waiting for me, no car load of heavies parked in the street.

It was twenty to ten when I got to Gordon's office. The covers were still on the typewriters and the girls were still yawning and comparing their engagement rings.

Diane said Gordon would be a little late. I said I would wait. I took the chair in front of her desk. I couldn't see her knees for the bit of the desk they call the modesty board. I don't know why she was being modest but I needed to concentrate on what I was going to say, so I watched her top half and tried not to look like a disgusting little man.

Gordon was late all right. He didn't turn up until half past ten. And I couldn't get a word with him on his own because he had Mrs Gunning with him.

He gave me an old-fashioned look and I followed them into his room. Mrs Gunning was wearing the brown dress, white gloves and plain black shoes. Her red hair was in a big bunch with a pony-tail tied by a small white bow.

'It was you who phoned my wife this morning, wasn't it?' he said, eyeing me coldly. 'I wish you wouldn't ring me at home. Mrs Gunning tells me you also phoned her – she says you've got some hare-brained scheme for breaking into the hospital and that I shouldn't be told about it? Is that right?'

'Look, could I have a word with you for a moment?' I said, trying to signal to him that it was important for us to be on our own.

'As Mrs Gunning is affected I don't see why she shouldn't hear,' he said. 'I pay you to carry out certain functions, not to start interfering in matters that don't concern you. Is that understood? She is the client and I am her solicitor and you are an inquiry operative and the sooner we all accept our roles the better. After what she's told me about your suggestion of breaking into St Margaret's Hospital I must seriously reconsider the whole question of whether this firm can go on employing you in any capacity.'

I turned to look at her.

'Mrs Gunning was shocked by my proposal, was she?' I said.

'I've told Mr Gregory all about it,' she said. Her eyes didn't even flick about a bit!

'So it's no good giving my side of it, is it?' I said to Gordon.

'I'd be interested to hear what kind of an explanation you'd come up with but I don't have time,' he said. 'Is it true or not?'

'I did put the idea up to her,' I said. I shrugged. 'I wanted to see how she'd react. As I guessed she jumped at it. She told you this morning I take it? Yeah, why didn't she tell you straight after I'd suggested it the other night – at dinner?'

Gordon looked at her. Cool as all get out she said:

'I should've told you yesterday, Mr Gregory, but I knew you'd be upset and I didn't want to make a serious accusation against Hazell that might cost him his job until I was sure. Then he phoned me this morning.'

'I see.' Gordon looked at me coldly. He tapped his fingers on the desk and then sat down. 'I'm afraid, James, this is too serious for me to ignore. I don't think I can jeopardize the firm's reputation by employing your services. Would you wait outside please?'

'He's sacking me,' I said to Mrs Gunning. 'I wish you'd tell him what I actually said to you on the phone this morning.'

'I've already told him. You wanted more money and – '

'Yeah, yeah, okay.' I turned away from Gordon's desk but I didn't head for the door. I sat down in the low clubman's arm-chair at the other end of the desk. Mrs Gunning had her ankles demurely crossed and her knees pressed together. She looked cool and matronly.

'I asked you to wait outside,' Gordon snapped.

'I know. You know if I'd done everything I was told I'd be a detective inspector today? I'd still be married to a beautiful wife? I might even have kids of my own?'

'For God's sake, James, will you get the hell out of – '

'No. I don't like to interfere in matters that don't concern me but sometimes you get involved without trying. Could I have a word with Mrs Gunning – in private?'

'No! Now kindly leave this office and – '

'Mrs Gunning?' I said.

She looked at him but he shook his head. He got up and went to the door and held it open.

'You want the whole office to hear?' I said. 'Okay by me. Mrs Gunning, I'll just ask you one question. Don't you think it would save everybody a lot of grief if you just forgot this whole affair and went back to your husband and child in Los Angeles?' I said the next bit slowly. 'Everything's bound to come out, you know.'

'What a stupid thing to say,' she snapped. 'Why don't you do what he says and disappear?'

Gordon was still standing there, dramatically holding the door open for me to scurry off, but as I was stuck to my club-man's chair he only looked silly.

When I think back on it I give myself a lot of praise for how I handled myself that morning. I mean, I'm supposed to be the disgusting *little* man who hangs about with *awful* gangsters.

'You can't go back to your husband and child, Mrs Gunning, can you?' I said, as gently as possible.

She knew then but still she tried to keep it up.

Poor Georgina, I was thinking.

'Close the door, Gordon,' I said, 'let's keep this among the three of us.' I waited until he came back to his desk. I couldn't tell anything from his face but the very fact that he wasn't calling three or four tea-girls to bounce me down the stairs showed that he was beginning to have doubts.

'Mrs Gunning didn't tell us that her little girl died after the car accident,' I said. 'It must've been a terrible shock for you and I didn't want to come out with it like this. That's why I was trying to phone everybody this morning. Your Helen is dead, Mrs Gunning, so there won't be any swapping of children, will there?'

I had on my sympathetic face. For a snooper I thought I was being almost saintly.

My Christ, had I underestimated *her*!

'I know all about that,' Gordon said. His voice was icy. 'Mrs Gunning has already told me.'

'When?'

'That doesn't matter, I know what the situation is and it doesn't make any difference to Mrs Gunning's claim for care and custody of Tricia Abrey. In fact, if you're going to run off to tell them all this I suggest you warn them that in my professional opinion this only makes Mrs Gunning's claim more likely to succeed. Without the complications of having to wrestle with the problem of the two children the whole matter is clear-cut. We are talking only about Patricia Abrey now. Living in that place, the father being unemployed, I should say that any judge will rule that the child's future will be immeasurably improved by a change in the parental situation. In fact, James, you can pass on another tit-bit. I'll admit that I did have some doubts about this case when there were two children to be considered but I have none now and I shall pursue Mrs Gunning's claim with all the energy and professional skill at my command. Without, I may add, the dubious advantage of your help.'

'Yeah,' said Mrs Gunning, giving me the most diabolical looks, 'and if you have any conscience at all you have another look at that dump and ask yourself if she was your child would you leave her to rot there – or get a chance of a new life!'

I stood up.

'I'm sorry for you, honestly I am,' I said quietly to Mrs Gunning.

I was.

I regretted it a lot that I was going to have to destroy her there and then, in public. Or semi-public, if Gordon didn't throw the door open again.

Chapter Fourteen

When I picked up the phone Gordon shot out a wrist as thin as a raspberry cane and tried to take it away from me.

He was cleverer than to keep trying once his long fingers found they could make no impression.

'I'm going to ask the international operator to get us a Los Angeles number,' I said.

'My God, I'll have you –'

'You'll know the number I mean, Mrs Gunning. Seven-six-five-zero-zero – you know the one, don't you? You ought to. I've never really been sure, are they ahead of us or behind us over there? Never mind, if your husband isn't at home we can try later. Hello – international operator, I wonder if you could get me a Los Angeles number – seven-six-five-zero –'

'Okay, you win,' said Mrs Gunning.

I held the phone away from my mouth and looked down at her.

'Sure?' I said.

'Yeah.'

'What is this all about?' Gordon demanded.

'Sorry, operator, I'll call again sometime,' I said, putting down the phone. Her head was downcast, her sun-tanned hands clasped on her lap, finger and thumb of the right hand working at the gold wedding ring on her left. It was the only ring she was wearing.

I supposed she'd thought the plain mother image would be better than the loud show biz.

She was no idiot.

'Mrs Gunning had better tell you,' I said.

'Okay,' she said. She looked up. Her face was remarkably composed. She didn't flinch from looking Gordon straight in the eye. 'I suppose I was crazy to think I could do it. He's obviously found out – ' she nodded at me – 'so I'd better come clean with you. After Helen died I had a breakdown and I guess Alan and I realized we didn't have much else but Helen. We've split up.'

For a moment Gordon had on that sad bloodhound face you see round bedsides in the incurables hospital. He forgot Eton enough to mutter something rude. He even slapped his desk.

'You're separated!' he exclaimed. 'Why in the name of – for God's sake, why didn't you tell me before we wasted all this time and effort? You do know that you've no chance now of being awarded custody of the child. As a happily married couple your chances were slim enough but . . .'

'That's why I didn't tell you,' she said quietly. 'I was hoping – well, maybe I was hoping if I looked like getting Patricia back it would bring us together again. I'm sorry I took up so much of your time – I also want to apologize to Mr Hazell, he did phone me this morning and say he couldn't possibly break into the hospital. I guess I've made a real fool of myself. I can only say I was shattered by what happened to Helen, I just couldn't think of anything but getting her back, I mean, Patricia. I'll naturally pay whatever you ask. I'm genuinely sorry.'

The strange thing was that I felt guilty.

'Well, Mrs Gunning,' he began, 'I – there's nothing useful I can say, is there? I think I know what you've been going through. I just hope that things – well – take a turn for the better.'

'Thank you,' she said, humbly.

'I can have the bill drawn up in five minutes – would you like it sent round to the hotel?' he said.

That made me feel a whole lot better.

We were back to normal.

'No, I'll settle right now,' she said. 'Will traveller's cheques be okay?'

As she got the cheques out of her bag Gordon nodded and we drifted out into Diane's office. Through the open door I could see the back of Mrs Gunning's red head and the end of the pen moving jerkily.

'I may owe you something of an apology, James,' he murmured, looking down his nose at me.

'No, you owe me about twenty hours at five guineas each.'

'However I don't want you to ring my house again. All right?'

The bastard meant it!

I was as near to sticking one on him then as made no difference.

Luckily our glaring session was interrupted by Georgina's quiet voice from the open doorway of Gordon's room.

'Just before I go,' she was saying, 'there's something I'd like to ask you.'

I stood my ground but Gordon went towards her. I looked a bit supid standing there with my dander up, facing up to an opponent who'd gone away. Creamy Diane gave me a knowing smile. I stood in the door of Gordon's room and tried to look menacing yet cool.

'I think I also owe the Abreys an apology,' Georgina was saying, apologetically. 'I'd really like to go and see them before I leave London. Do you think – I mean, they know why I was here – would they –'

'I don't think it would be a good idea at all,' Gordon said coldly.

The bastard looked at his watch!

And I was supposed to be a hard, disgusting, little man?

'I'd just like to say sorry to them – and see Patricia once,' she said, pleading with him.

'I am no longer your legal adviser and I can't stop you but if you want my opinion I should advise you most strongly against visiting them. I think they'd be most resentful – and one cannot really see why they shouldn't be.'

'I see,' she said, her face falling. 'Good-bye then.'

They shook hands. Gordon's mind was already on something else. As she left his room I stood back to let her past. Our eyes met but we didn't shake hands.

'Yeah well, I'll be seeing you later I daresay,' I said to Gordon.

'Yes,' he said curtly, looking up briefly.

I didn't start hurrying until I was out in the corridor but she'd already gone down in a lift. I saw the lights going on as it stopped at each floor.

I ran down the six flights, three steps at a time.

She was just stepping off the kerb to tell the taxi-driver where to go when I came rushing out of the front entrance.

'It's all right, I've got the car,' I said, pushing the cab door shut again.

'You wanna cab or donchyer, missus?' barked the driver.

'She don't,' I said.

With some polished remark or another he drove off.

'I'll take you to see the Abreys,' I said. 'It'll be all right, they're decent people really.'

'Thanks,' she said.

Poor Georgina.

That's what I was thinking.

Don't be fooled, I wasn't getting soft. Taking her there to make her apologies was just about the only thing I could do to make Toni take that spit back.

And that's what I wanted more than anything else, before or since.

As we drove through the City Georgina didn't say much but she kept twisting round in her seat.

'Taking a last look at the old place, eh?' I said.

'No, I want to buy something.'

We were in Whitechapel when she suddenly told me to stop. I watched her go into the shop. Poor Georgina, I kept saying to myself.

After six or seven minutes she reappeared, struggling with a parcel so big it was going to be difficult to get it into the car. I got out to help her.

'What've you got in there?' I asked. It was a big, solid parcel, wrapped in brown paper.

'You forgotten?' she said.

'Forgotten what?'

'August the sixth.'

'So what?'

'It's Patricia's birthday.' She gave a guilty smile.

I opened the passenger door and we manoeuvred the birthday present into the seat and then into the back.

It took us another ten minutes to reach Herbert Morrison House. The three of us, Georgina, myself and the brown paper parcel, crushed into the lift.

As we came towards the Abreys' door we could hear a lot of noise from inside, children's voices mainly.

'Don't expect open arms,' I said.

'Don't worry about me.'

I don't know why but I was worried about what poor Georgina was going to go through.

Poor Georgina!

Poor stupid Jim Hazell!

I rang the bell three times before anyone came to the door. It was Cliff. He was wearing a tall clown's hat and paper streamers round his neck. He was grinning brightly, until he saw us. Then his teeth vanished.

'You've got a fucking – ' he began.

I didn't let him finish.

'Look, I've got something very important to tell you,' I said. I took him by the arm and led him a few steps away from Mrs Gunning. He didn't want to come but I am fairly strong.

He might have put up more of a battle only he kept looking over his shoulder at Georgina.

'That's her, innit?' he demanded. 'This had better be good you – '

'Listen. I've got her to forget the whole business. Got that? *It's all forgotten.* She's going back to America. All she wants is to see Tricia just the once, to give her a birthday present.'

His eyes were staring at mine. There wasn't much space between our faces. I thought the hat and the streamers looked terrible on him.

'You expect me to believe that – after what you was telling us?' he growled.

'You got my word on it. She understands that it's not on. It wouldn't do you any harm would it?'

He stared back over his shoulder.

She had on her bereaved face.

'You'd better be on the level this time or I'll kill you, my life I will.'

I nodded. What was another stray threat of murder, to a man like me?

'You going home to America?' he growled at Georgina.

'Yes. In the morning. I made a mistake. If I could say to your wife how sorry I am – I brought this for your little girl . . .'

'Stay here,' he said, 'I'll see Toni.'

We both stood in the corridor not looking at each other for about ten minutes. It was obvious Toni wasn't too thrilled with the idea of the smash and grab mob turning up again. It sounded as if the kids were having a great party.

Cliff came to the door again.

'Come through to the kitchen,' he mumbled.

I let Georgina go in first. There must have been about twenty children. The living-room table had been pushed against the wall. On it were the remnants of the party tea. They hadn't left much, a few half-eaten sandwiches, some jelly and custard strewn across the table-cloth, and some bits of brown cake still stuck to wrinkled paper. One small boy was doing his best not to leave anything, including the bits of sandwiches.

A large, jolly woman was organizing a game in the middle of the room to Pinky and Perky music on a record-player.

Toni was standing in the little kitchenette, Tricia by her side. She was holding the kid's hand, very tightly. Cliff turned and for a moment the Abrey family faced us defiantly. Georgina looked as if she was ready to break down.

'Happy birthday, Tricia,' I said, 'this is your Aunty Georgina, she's got a present for you.'

What else could I say? Cliff and Toni weren't racing to do the introductions.

Georgina pushed the big package at Tricia. She tried to speak but the words choked on her.

As Tricia started to tear at the brown paper I looked at Toni. She didn't blink or look away or even blush. She stared at me with contempt.

Georgina crouched down as Tricia demolished the brown

paper wrapping. I didn't dare look at Cliff's face. The two heads were almost touching – and the red hair was exactly the same shade.

It was a bright yellow teddy bear, a good twelve inches taller than little Tricia. She threw her arms round Georgina's neck and both heads of red hair became one.

'Thank you, oh thank you Aunt Georgina,' Tricia said breathlessly, 'it's my best present, it's lovely, oh thank you.'

She started to drag it into the living-room, shouting to her little friends.

'You shouldn't have,' Cliff growled at Georgina, without looking her directly in the face, 'them big teddies will set you back a score at least.'

'It's nothing,' said Georgina. She looked at Toni. The kids were squealing and her voice was low but I heard what she said. 'I'm really sorry, Toni.'

Then she turned. She pushed her way through the little crowded living-room, waist-deep in children. I watched her put her hand on Tricia's head and bend down to kiss her and then she was gone.

'Yeah well,' said Cliff, looking at Toni's face and then mine. 'Nice of her, wasn't it, Toni?'

'Her own child died,' I said. 'She wanted just to come this once, you didn't mind, I hope?'

'No, I suppose not,' said Cliff, looking uncertainly at Toni.

'You won't be wanting to join in the party games so you'll be off now,' Toni said, her voice well under control but very, very bitter.

'She didn't want to – ' I began. What was the use? Once you've been caught out in one lie you're always a liar . . .

I drove Mrs Gunning back to Claridges and said I hoped she'd get over it and watched her go in the front entrance and then I drove slowly down to Bond Street, turned right for Piccadilly and thought what a sad world this is.

I heard the horns hooting angrily for some seconds before I realized they were meaning me. The lights at the bottom of Haymarket had changed to green but I'd been lost in my sad thoughts.

One of the cars behind slowed as it pulled alongside me. The driver had stiff grey hair and a shirt with blue stripes. I'll always remember that guy.

'You stupid bastard,' he roared out of his window and then shot away along Pall Mall.

I was quite near him at the next red but I didn't get out and walk over and drag him out of the car.

In fact I was quite grateful to him. Kiddies' playtime was over. It was almost six o'clock. Time for me to plunge back into the big, hard, grown-up world.

Sure as rain in Manchester Keith O'Rourke would be coming round tonight.

Chapter Fifteen

It was nine o'clock when I heard the knock downstairs.

I was stretched on the big leather couch in the lounge, the television on with the sound almost off, a bottle of coke propped on my chest, the Luger on the rug.

I let the bottle fall as I slid off the couch and crossed the big room quickly and put off the lights.

They hammered again at the front door.

'It's open,' I shouted down the stairs. Then I moved quickly across the landing and got my back to the wall. They knocked again. I leaned over the banister and shouted again. 'It's open, come on up.'

I heard the door hitting the inside wall. A man's voice said:

'Where the hell are you?'

'Up here,' I called.

I waited until the feet had come half-way up the stairs, then I switched on the light and lifted the gun.

It was aimed right on the back of his neck.

Only it wasn't Keith O'Rourke's neck.

I'd have known that black, greasy hair anywhere!

'What the hell?' I said, dropping the gun to my side.

Cliff Abrey's pale face peered up at me. I went round to the top of the stairs. He may have seen the gun, he may not. But he kept on coming up.

'What are you –'

'Where the hell is she, you bastard?' he shouted. He was on the top step but one.

'Where's who?'

'Tricia, you bastard,' he shouted. Then he came towards me and before I could lift a hand he belted me in the face.

I staggered back into the open door of the darkened fish-room.

He came jumping at me again, his pale face rigid with anger.

'I'll fucking swing for you,' he was yelling. 'Where's Tricia? If you don't tell me – '

I put up my left hand to ward him off but he came at me all ways, kicking and kneeing, both fists swinging at my face.

He was no fighter but I had a gun in my right hand and he was stronger than I would have thought and he'd taken me by surprise. I tried to push him away with my left hand while I poked the gun into my hip pocket. It kept sticking. I couldn't just drop it in case he got hold of it, he was mad enough to shoot me without blinking. We wrestled in the soft purple light of the fish tanks.

The gun wouldn't go into my hip pocket. I ducked his wild swings and he kicked at my ankles. Then he was coming at me with a chair. I put up my left arm to shield my head. It hit me down the arm and banged my ear.

He swung the chair high again and whooshed it down at me. I jumped to one side. The chair hit the fish tanks with a terrible cracking noise and water spouted out on to my back.

Then the pistol slipped into my hip pocket.

I ducked to the left and feinted with my head and before he could free the chair from the metal frame of the tank I buried my right fist into his stomach.

He started to bend forward. It seemed to be happening in slow motion. I grabbed him by the scruff of the neck and twisted his head back, his neck across my thigh.

He was gasping to breathe. Funny noises were coming from his throat. Something, a flashing movement, caught my eye. I let him drop.

He lay there groaning and trying to retch.

A couple of fish were jumping on the carpet beside his feet. Reggie's paradise fish!

Jesus Christ!

It's not easy to catch one of these small fish when it's leaping about for dear life on a smooth carpet and you're having to step over the legs of a man who might be jumping at your throat any minute.

And when I had the little brutes in my hand I found their

tank was dry. He'd smashed the whole front in. They were wriggling in my hand.

The hell with it, killers or not, they had to go somewhere. I lifted the lid of the next tank with the muzzle of the gun and lobbed them into the water.

It was the tank with the pair of giant Oscars. But I didn't have time to see how the giants handled the deadly little killers.

'You up there, Jim?' came a shout from downstairs.

I dropped to one knee beside Cliff.

'You stay on the floor and don't make a bloody sound,' I said. 'These guys are real killers and they'll see you off double-quick. I hope you bloody understand.'

I came out of the fish-room in a crouch and hit the light switch on the landing. For a moment the only sound was the gurgling of the tanks.

'Is James Hazell at home?' said the man's voice. Another man laughed.

'Yeah, that you?' I said, 'come on up. Shut the door behind you.'

'Shut the door, there's a good lad,' said Keith O'Rourke.

'Bleeding dark in here, innit?' said the other one.

The idea had been to take Keith on the stairs and put a bullet through his legs.

But Cliff had spoiled all that.

I waited till the two of them were almost at the top of the stairs, then I switched on the light.

Keith had the sawn-off shotgun at chest-height. He was staring up the stairs, his gloved finger on the trigger. I raised the pistol. But before I could speak Cliff said something in the fish-room.

Keith jumped to the top of the stairs and pointed the shotgun into the half-lit room.

'Hallo, Jim,' he said cheerily, 'just come to blow your fucking head off, haven't I?'

He got the butt against his shoulder and his hand tightened on the trigger guard. I could have winged him but he would only have come back.

I shot him right through the head; in that enclosed space it was like a bomb going off. As he hit the opposite wall his mate let out a yelp.

I leaned over the banister, took steady aim and fired at his backside.

I saw the hole in his trousers and then he screamed and half-fell, half-scrambled back down the stairs, dropping his sawn-off on the stair rug.

Cliff Abrey stood in the doorway of the fish-room his mouth gaping at the sight of Keith's blood making abstract patterns on the nice wallpaper.

'You shot him!' he squeaked.

'That's right.'

'He was going to shoot me! Why?'

'Just remember that when the cops come. He was going to shoot you. What were you saying about Tricia?'

'She's gone,' he said, 'I'm going to be sick.'

'What do you mean, gone?'

'We let her out in the – ohhhh . . .'

He turned away and spewed into the purplish darkness of the fish-room.

Chapter Sixteen

'I ain't ever seen a – dead person before,' Cliff moaned, between gulps and gasps. I got him into the big lounge and let him collapse on the leather couch. His mouth was hanging loose and his eyes were dull and the noises coming from his deep throat didn't sound too healthy for the carpet.

'We won't have long so tell me what's happened to Tricia,' I said, tapping his foot with my toe.

'I'm going to be sick again,' he wailed.

'She's missing, is she? Come on, you berk, that guy's better off dead. He'd have killed both of us. What about Tricia?'

Give him credit, his stomach was trying to hit the ceiling but he clenched his fists and took a deep breath.

'She was in the playground with two of her little mates – '

'When?'

'About half past seven. They was kids from the block, she only got to know them at the birthday party yesterday, Toni's always saying we oughter let her play down there and this other mum's only on the second floor and she said she'd keep an eye on 'em. She said she was only in the other room a coupla minutes and then she can't see any of them and the other comes running up the stairs and says a woman come and took Tricia for a car-ride, it was her Aunty – '

'Georgina?'

'Yeah – red hair and smart clothes.'

'So that was about two hours ago. You tell the cops?'

'No. I thought you'd know all about it so I got the car and come over here.' He was breathing easier now and his face didn't look so green. He looked at me steadily. 'Toni knew about this place.'

'It was on my card,' I said, 'yeah, I'd written it on the back.'

'Oh that's how, was it? I oughter call the law now then. You didn't have anything to do with it then?'

'Course I bloody didn't. But don't tell the law. I'm going to call them now about him out there on the landing.'

'We gotta tell them about Trish!'

'You tell the cops about Georgina snatching Tricia and it'll be on every front page tomorrow. The whole story will come out. You want that? For the rest of your lives you'll all be marked, the whole bloody world will be looking at you and Toni and saying Tricia wasn't your kid!'

'I don't care – we've got to get her back!'

'You'll get her back, I promise. Did the kids say if she was in a taxi?'

'No, a blue car they said.'

'She must've hired it. That means she planned it. What does she expect you to do? Call the cops, first thing. That means the airports and the docks would be watched. No, she won't try to leave the country, I'll bet on it.'

'But she could go anywhere!'

'Yeah? With a six-year-old who's screaming for her mummy? She's going to have to hide away somewhere, isn't she? Counting on you to raise the alarm. She can't get the kid through the law so now she's going to chuck it to the newspapers. You get it?'

'I don't fucking know – where the hell's she gone, that's all I care about.'

'I think I might just know. Now I'm going to make two calls. One to Alan Gunning in Los Angeles, one to the law. Old Bill's bound to be here before we get through to Los Angeles. Whatever happens one of us has got to speak to Alan Gunning – ask him what the address is of the bungalow in Broadstairs. You got that? The bungalow in Broadstairs. And not a word to the cops, right? She wants it to get out, don't you see?'

'I don't, no –'

'Get yourself a drink while I start phoning. And don't worry, she won't hurt Tricia. She thinks she's her little girl. Tricia will be all right.'

I started dialling. I watched him going unsteadily to the bar.

Through the open door I could see Keith O'Rourke's back, his left arm twisted behind him, little points of light shining on the dark red mess of his hair.

When I'd made the two calls. I put down the phone. Cliff was still looking down uncertainly at the rows of fancy bottles under Reggie's bar.

'I generally have a tonic water from the fridge,' I said.

'Oh yeah, ta.'

We both heard the gurgling noise at the same time.

Cliff's eyes opened wide. His head shot round.

'It's okay, it's his pipes rumbling,' I said, 'All of you doesn't die at the same time you know.'

He didn't know and he looked ready to throw up at the news.

'Give me over a bottle of that stuff, will you?' I said, standing by the phone. It wasn't till he brought it over that I realized I still had the Luger in my right hand. I put it on the phone table.

'I'm gambling she's taken Tricia to this bungalow,' I said. 'She'd have expected you to get on to the cops straight away. They'd have warned London Airport first off. Her husband bought this bungalow for her mother. I'm betting she won't remember telling me about it.'

'But what does she think she's going to do – with Tricia?'

'She's clever enough to know she can't keep her – every police force in the world would be looking out for her. My guess is she just wants to have Tricia to herself for a few days. She might even have the crazy idea she can convince Tricia she's her real mother.'

He shuddered.

'It'll be all right,' I said. 'The sooner we get this mess sorted out the better. Just remember the main thing – he came here with a shotgun and you heard him saying he was going to blow my head off. Right?'

'Yeah, he did say that. What was he going to blow your head off for?'

'We were at school together and I nicked his marbles.'

He nodded weakly. It was all too much for him but he was trying to keep going.

I didn't tell him we were gambling on Tricia's life.

The phone rang as the squad car pulled up outside the house.

'Go downstairs and keep 'em talking,' I snapped, snatching up the phone. Cliff nodded and went down to the front door. I closed my eyes and said a little wish.

'Alan Gunning,' said the clear, cockney voice in Los Angeles. I heard them talking at the front door.

'Mr Gunning, my name's James Hazell and I'm phoning you from London,' I said, forcing myself to sound like a man who didn't have cops coming up the stairs to ask him about the spattered blood on the landing wallpaper. 'I'm phoning about your wife, Georgina. I don't have much time – I'll explain it later but it's really very urgent. Can you tell me the address of the bungalow you bought for your mother-in-law in Broadstairs?'

'Why, wot's it about? Where's Georgina?'

'She's taken someone else's baby and I think she's gone to that bungalow. I want to get her before they call in the law. You follow?'

They were at the top of the stairs now. Two of them came into the lounge, staring at me with hard eyes. I pointed to the phone and then to the gun on the little table.

'Who are you then, cock?' Gunning asked.

'I work for her solicitors. It's really most urgent – the address.'

'Could you finish your call, sir?' barked one of the CID men.

'It's from Los Angeles,' I said, my hand over the mouthpiece. 'Won't be a sec. Nothing to do with that out there.'

'I suggest you ring your party back, sir,' he snapped, making a move to take the phone from my hand.

I turned my back on him.

'Please, Mr Gunning, the address,' I said. 'It's urgent.'

The plainclothes man took hold of the phone.

'Who is this calling?' he said, one of the new generation, longish hair and clothes that didn't come from under the carpet. He listened to whatever Alan Gunning was saying.

'I am a police officer, sir, would you care to give me your

number? . . .' He shifted the phone to his left hand and brought out a wire-bound notebook and a smart ballpoint. I could only stand there and watch. 'And what did Mr Hazell phone you about, sir?' He put the notebook on the table beside the Luger and leaned over, writing in neat capitals. 'No, sir, I'm afraid Mr Hazell can't speak to you now. He may be able to ring you back later . . . he was phoning you about a house you wanted to buy in Ellerslie Crescent? . . . no, sir, I can't tell you anything at present . . . yes, sir . . no, I'm sorry, we don't have time for that now, sir . . . you can tell him about your wife later . . . yes well that's not what we're here about, sir . . . I can't do that either, sir . . .'

I looked at Cliff, my head moving slightly from side to side. He blinked two or three times. The young plainclothes sergeant put down the phone.

'It was a call to a man in Los Angeles,' he said to the older detective. 'I don't think it had anything to do with this. I've got his number.'

And I had the address in Broadstairs. Alan Gunning had found a way of telling me. You can't keep a good cockney down! If only Cliff could keep quiet . . .

They tried it on for size every way. They grilled us separately in the house and at the station. I kept telling them that Keith O'Rourke had threatened violence on my person.

They didn't show any reaction. If anything they seemed more suspicious of me, an ex-cop on good terms with a Flying Squad bloke, living in a fraud merchant's house, being threatened by a newly-released con.

They wanted to know about Cliff. Why had we been fighting?

'I've been working on a custody claim involving his daughter. The firm of solicitors are Venables, Venables, Williams and Gregory. He was a bit roused and decided to have a go at me. He had nothing to do with O'Rourke. Phone Gordon Gregory, he's a senior partner, he'll tell you.'

Why didn't I phone the police when O'Rourke broke in?

'I didn't have time. Abrey must have left the door on the latch. Soon as I heard the voice downstairs I knew it was

O'Rourke. Detective Inspector Minty had warned me he was telling people he wanted to sort me out.'

But I'd just happened to have a gun? That was a bit suspicious, wasn't it?

'I knew Mancini had it hidden in the gravel of one of the fish tanks. When Abrey came hammering at the door I thought he was O'Rourke and I got it out of the tank. I don't even think you can get me for illegal possession, can you? It was Mancini's gun. What else was I supposed to do when a villain like O'Rourke turned up with a shotgun?'

All right, but why shoot him through the head? You didn't have to kill him, did you?

'He was going to let off the shotgun at Abrey. He said, "Hullo, Jim, I've come to blow your fucking head off". I was standing at the other end of the landing. He got the shotgun up and was going to let Abrey have it. That room with the fish was almost dark, only the lights from the tank, he didn't know it was Abrey. I didn't have time to think, he was going to shoot Abrey who had nothing to do with it, so I let him have it. I'm not all that good a marksman. I had a shot at the other one, I think I got him in the arse.'

Mr Minty says O'Rourke didn't know where you were living. How did he find out? You set up the whole thing, did you?

'You joking? Think I'm a bleeding master-mind? You send a car round to see Mum and Dad, they'll tell you how he must have found out where I was living. He was round at their house in Haggerston the other night. He was a nutter. They didn't tell him. I wasn't sitting there waiting for him.'

Yet you got the pistol out quick enough when Abrey came hammering at the door?

'Well, of course. O'Rourke had been putting the frighteners on Mum and the old man, who else would he have been asking? Quite a few people could've told him. Mancini could've told anybody in Parkhurst, couldn't he? So I wasn't taking any chances.'

Abrey says the door was open when he came to the house. That's funny, isn't it, expecting a heavy team and you leave the door on the latch?

'Just shows you, doesn't it? Would I have been that careless if I'd been really expecting O'Rourke? That door always swings shut, it's pretty heavy. I just didn't remember I hadn't locked it.'

Who was the other man with O'Rourke?

I didn't recognize him. You could start looking for some geezer with his reggie in bandages. He had a shotgun as well.'

We know that, it was on the stairs. You still say you didn't deliberately aim to kill him?

'No, I just let fly. If I'd been facing him I might have tried talking but you know what it's like when a bloke's ready to blast off, you make a sudden move and he's liable just to swing round and blast off.'

You should know that, with your police experience. Why did you leave the Met?

'I got my ankle smashed by a wages gang in Fulham, about eighteen months ago. It was going to take a long time to heal and I got fed up sitting around drawing sick pay. My wife left me as well, I was drinking a bit – I dunno, I just didn't have the stomach for it any more.'

You seem to have got the stomach for it tonight in no uncertain fashion.

'Yeah, well, there you go.'

Okay, we're letting you go now. There may be charges, it'll have to go higher. Can't have citizens shooting each other dead all over the shop, can we?

'I was only having a go.'

Nobody's going to miss O'Rourke, that's for sure.

It was five in the morning when they let us out. They offered to drive us back to Reggie's house but I said if they got a taxi I'd see Cliff home to Bethnal Green.

The young detective-sergeant came past the desk as we were waiting for the taxi to come.

'There you go,' he said cheerily. Then he stopped. 'By the way, that bloke you were talking to on the phone, Mr Gunning was it? He said to tell you his wife had a bad breakdown and tried to kill herself a couple of times. He said she'd have to be treated gently for a while, she's a bit disturbed. I said I'd pass on the message.'

It took Cliff a moment or two to get it.

'What?' he said, panic flashing across his tired, pale face.

'It's okay,' I said. I had him by the arm, my fingers digging right through to the bone.

He started to struggle as we were getting into the taxi.

'You heard him,' he started shouting, 'she's off her head, she's tried to kill herself – '

'So let's get a move on,' I snapped, shoving him into the back of the taxi.

'But if she's off her head – ' he yelped, struggling to get free.

'She had a bit of a breakdown when her kid died, that's all,' I said calmly.

Alan Gunning had been trying to warn me. But I'd known already. It was one of the things Jonathon Bowles had found out. The death of her little girl had torn Georgina apart. She'd tried to kill herself a couple of times.

I didn't allow myself to think of what that poor, desperate bitch might decide to do with herself and Tricia rather than face the rest of her life without the only baby she was ever going to have.

Chapter Seventeen

Herbert Morrison House was a giant cornflake box against a pink dawn sky.

I kept the engine running and waited for Cliff to come back out of the front entrance.

It took him four and a half minutes and the reason he wasn't quicker was that Toni had come with him.

I got out on the pavement.

'She's coming as well,' he called as they started to run across the wide, empty street.

'So what if Tricia turns up at the house?' I said, scowling.

'Mrs Harris from next door is going to wait in our place in case she comes back,' said Toni. 'I've said we'll ring her.'

'You aren't on the phone,' I said.

'Mrs Harris is.'

Of course I didn't want Toni to come with us. I'm not that cool. Sitting with both of them in the car for an hour or more? After all that had happened between us?

'I tried to stop her,' Cliff said, apologetically.

Knowing that this was the last time I'd ever be near her?

'Come on, let's move,' I snapped.

I held the door open.

Cliff got in the back before I could stop him. I could have shoved his good manners down his throat but I got in and Toni slammed the passenger door and I whipped off the handbrake and we belted through Bethnal Green.

Nobody spoke until we were swishing through the Dartford Tunnel.

'You got change for the toll?' I said.

Neither of them had a penny. I started feeling in my jacket pockets.

Then we were onto the M2 motorway and I couldn't see any police patrols and I thought what the hell and I cracked down on the motor and the needle went round to 120. Miles per hour.

And Toni said nothing.

The signs came and went before I could blink, Chatham, Rainham, Sittingbourne, Whitstable, Herne Bay, and then we were slowing down and I started looking for a friendly local bobby to direct us to Ellerslie Crescent, Broadstairs.

A man cycling to work with a gas-mask case slung round his shoulder and his big labourer's boots sticking out from the pedals gave us a rough idea.

'Thanks mate,' I called, revving the Stag away so fast he seemed to wobble in our slipstream.

Then we saw a boy with a newspaper satchel. Funny, I didn't think they still had paperboys.

He showed us the way to Ellerslie Crescent.

'It's a dead end, Mister,' he said. 'You'll see the cul-de-sac sign.'

'You know if there's any empty bungalows in the street?' I said. 'I mean, been empty for a good long time?'

'I think there is, at the other end, where it stops at the cliff.'

'Cheers,' I said.

Cliff had pulled himself forward on the back seat, his face peering between Toni and me.

'He said a cliff!' His voice was anxious but I made a noise like a laugh and said the cliffs about here weren't high enough to worry about.

I presumed I was lying. I didn't know the cliffs at Broadstairs but I had told so many lies I couldn't imagine myself ever telling the truth again.

It took us an hour and fifteen minutes to get from Bethnal Green to Broadstairs. But it took us half an hour to find that bungalow. The crescent was deserted and I didn't want to create any hullabaloo by waking the neighbours.

We drove up and down.

'I'll go in and ask somebody,' Toni said several times, each time sounding more panicky.

'Yeah, you get some of those retired gents out of their beds at this time and ask him where's the empty bungalow and what's he going to think? He'll phone the law and say there's a gang of London crooks looking for a hide-out.'

'Jim's right, Toni,' said Cliff.

'Well, I'm not sitting in this bloody car wasting time when – '

'Just shut up, Toni,' he barked.

Then I saw this old dear out in her front garden with a watering-can. I rolled the Stag into the kerb, told Cliff and Toni to sit there and keep quiet, and got out.

'Good morning, madam,' I said, looking over her hedge. 'I wonder if you can help me. I must say, you're up rather early, aren't you?'

She had a blue rinse, that's all I remember about her. My face was a pleasant smile and my guts were tight.

'You must water them before the sun's up,' she said. 'I like it in the early mornings, don't you? There's no noisy traffic, the air's so clean . . .'

Yeah yeah.

'Yes, you've got to be up early in the morning these days,' I said. 'My wife and I have been driving since four o'clock. I hope we're still in time, there's a house for sale in this crescent and we're trying to see it before the rush. You know how it is these days, we've been looking for ages.'

'The prices they're asking are absolutely ridiculous,' she said. 'Which one is it, I haven't heard of any being on the market.'

'It's a bungalow, I believe it's been empty for some time, but I've been up and down the street and I can't see any empty ones.'

'You must mean Mr Clement's old house, he's dead now, somebody did buy it but I've never seen them.'

'How do you get to it?'

She came out onto the pavement, a bowed old dear with a bright blue rinse and little brown arms. She had a look at the Stag and then she started pointing.

'We'll walk,' I said into the car.

The old dear was still hanging about her gate, waiting to get a look at my wife. I gave her a nice big smile. Toni got out. Then Cliff. The old dear kept watching us as we walked away.

I could see why Georgina's mother would not have fancied living alone in that house. It was hard to get at, being at the end of an unmade stretch of private road, and a lot of heavy bushes and trees cut it off from the rest of the crescent. You couldn't see it from the road.

I got a glimpse of the Thames estuary through a gap in a hedge. The water was smooth and blue. It was going to be a beautiful day.

'Okay,' I said, 'you two are going to wait here in these bushes.'

'No, I'm going in there to get Tricia,' said Toni.

'If she sees you she knows the game's up, right?'

'Yeah,' said Cliff.

'Don't worry,' I said to Toni. 'And keep out of sight until I let you know.'

'Just get her,' Toni said. It was the last time we ever spoke to each other.

I walked up the unmade road, walking steadily, making no attempt to hide. I got through the garden gate and up to the front door without hearing anything.

I gently lifted up the letterbox and got my ear against the gap. The house was silent.

I walked on the soft earth of the flower-beds to the corner. There was a garage and then a steep bank with a fence and bushes at the top, no room to squeeze through.

I walked on my own footprints along the front of the house to the other corner.

Roses were growing thick on a high trellis. I put my forefinger in amongst the leaves and stems and pushed them delicately to one side. I could see a bit of lawn stretching to a small bank with a low, neat fence of wire and concrete posts on top.

After that there was only sky and water.

That's when I heard a child's voice.

It was coming from the back of the house, the part I couldn't see.

I looked round quickly. The trellis work was built into a grassy bank. I reached up and took hold of a clump of grass and tried to pull myself up. The grass fell away from the bank, spattering bits of earth on my face and chest.

I licked my lips and spat silently. It had to be the garage way.

There was about six inches of space between the garage wall and the bank on that side of the house. I went in shoulder-first and kept the back of my head against the concrete wall.

Stones jagged into my stomach. Cobwebs stuck to my face. My shirt front tore on something.

Then I was at the end of the garage wall. Slowly I let my face edge to the corner.

'I don't want to go on the beach,' Tricia was saying.

'It's going to be a terrific day, love,' said a woman's cockney voice. 'We can have ice-lollies and – '

'My Daddy doesn't let me have ice-lollies, he says they're bad for my teeth.'

'He's silly, int he? Course you can have ice-lollies. I won't stop you having what you want.'

'I want to go home. You said Mummy and Daddy was coming here, it was going to be a surprise.'

'Well, we won't worry about them, will we? We're having a good time on our own, aren't we?'

I edged my nose round the corner.

Georgina was standing on the grass, looking at the door of the house. I couldn't see Tricia. I eased my stomach sideways. From the sound of her voice Tricia could only be standing a few feet away from Georgina.

It was about fifteen, maybe twenty yards to the little bank at the end of the garden, where the cliff was.

I lifted my right foot. There wasn't enough room to stand in that narrow gap without twisting my feet sideways.

'Wouldn't it be lovely, to live all the time where it was sunny?' Georgina said. She was smiling. Her arms were folded. Her red hair was hanging loose down her back.

'I want to go home,' Tricia said. She sounded more tired than afraid.

'We could have a house like this by the sea and we could go for sails and play on the beach – '

'I don't like boats.'

Georgina turned to point down the garden to the sea. She was half-smiling.

'Come on, Helen,' she said, 'let's walk down to the edge and watch the ships and you'll see how – '

'I'm not Helen, my name is Tricia,' said the little girl's indignant voice.

'Isn't Helen a nicer name? Come on, take my hand.'

I reached my right leg out, gave myself a push and came out of the narrow gap at a sprint.

Tricia was standing in the open door.

Georgina turned. When she saw me she started to run towards Tricia.

That was when my ankle gave way. It had been twisted sideways so long in the narrow gap it had lost all feeling. I saw mossy flagstones coming towards my face.

'Get in the house, Tricia,' I yelled, running at a scramble. I hit the door a fraction before Georgina and stretched out my arms, panting heavily.

'It's all right,' Georgina said, letting her shoulders fall, her face quivering with a sad little smile. I didn't move. 'Why are you standing there like that?'

She looked at me for a moment. Then the tears came into her eyes.

'Did you think I would hurt her?' she said. 'My little Helen?'

Chapter Eighteen

I never did get my five guineas an hour. That bastard Gordon said he'd added it up and I'd earned exactly what he'd loaned me.

It didn't take an Einstein brain to see this as a gentle hint that I was through with Venables, Venables, Williams and Gregory.

So I took Dot's Birmingham job. A tenner a day and luncheon vouchers. Still, she said if I behaved myself and showed promise she might find me something more suited to my talents. Like the great lemonade warehouse fiddle where I had to join up as a driver's mate and lug crates of soda-pop into every small shop between Battersea and Woking.

Alan Gunning turned up a day later and took Georgina home. He was a very decent bloke. He said he would see she got the best psychiatric help going.

I thought of telling him what I knew. He seemed genuine and I reckoned he might have felt it up to him to contribute some of his fortune to the Abreys.

But I didn't. They'd always have known why he was contributing. As it was everybody put the whole story down to Georgina's state of shock and hoped she would soon get better and stop having these crazy fantasies.

In the end the law didn't charge me with anything.

I tore up Nurse Drummond's notebooks.

I couldn't tear up the memory, worse luck. That weird little dark room and the woman with the straight back and the lonely, ugly face.

All those years working for other women and their babies and having nothing to look forward to but loneliness.

'It was like a madness,' said her voice in my memory, 'I hated that woman with the red hair, she called me an ugly old cow and I was so upset I took the tag and put it on the other baby and next morning when I came back on duty I was too frightened to tell anybody. I've known I'd be punished for it and I've been praying and I'm glad you've come at last.'

I'm a hard bastard, everybody knows that – but Solomon was going to cut the kid in half, wasn't he? All I did was try to make as few people unhappy as possible. What would you have done?

I often think I'd like to sneak into Herbert Morrison House and see how Toni is, and how Tricia is growing up but I never will. I can't even see the words Bethnal Green in a newspaper without feeling as if somebody's opened a big drain in the bottom of my stomach.

Discover more about our forthcoming books through Penguin's FREE newspaper...

Penguin Quarterly

It's packed with:

- exciting features
- author interviews
- previews & reviews
- books from your favourite films & TV series
- exclusive competitions & much, much more...

Write off for your free copy today to:
Dept JC
Penguin Books Ltd
FREEPOST
West Drayton
Middlesex
UB7 0BR
NO STAMP REQUIRED

READ MORE IN PENGUIN

In every corner of the world, on every subject under the sun, Penguin represents quality and variety – the very best in publishing today.

For complete information about books available from Penguin – including Puffins, Penguin Classics and Arkana – and how to order them, write to us at the appropriate address below. Please note that for copyright reasons the selection of books varies from country to country.

In the United Kingdom: Please write to *Dept. JC, Penguin Books Ltd, FREEPOST, West Drayton, Middlesex UB7 0BR*

If you have any difficulty in obtaining a title, please send your order with the correct money, plus ten per cent for postage and packaging, to *PO Box No. 11, West Drayton, Middlesex UB7 0BR*

In the United States: Please write to *Penguin USA Inc., 375 Hudson Street, New York, NY 10014*

In Canada: Please write to *Penguin Books Canada Ltd, 10 Alcorn Avenue, Suite 300, Toronto, Ontario M4V 3B2*

In Australia: Please write to *Penguin Books Australia Ltd, 487 Maroondah Highway, Ringwood, Victoria 3134*

In New Zealand: Please write to *Penguin Books (NZ) Ltd, 182–190 Wairau Road, Private Bag, Takapuna, Auckland 9*

In India: Please write to *Penguin Books India Pvt Ltd, 706 Eros Apartments, 56 Nehru Place, New Delhi 110 019*

In the Netherlands: Please write to *Penguin Books Netherlands B.V., Keizersgracht 231 NL–1016 DV Amsterdam*

In Germany: Please write to *Penguin Books Deutschland GmbH, Friedrichstrasse 10–12, W–6000 Frankfurt/Main 1*

In Spain: Please write to *Penguin Books S. A., C. San Bernardo 117–6° E–28015 Madrid*

In Italy: Please write to *Penguin Italia s.r.l., Via Felice Casati 20, I–20124 Milano*

In France: Please write to *Penguin France S. A., 17 rue Lejeune, F–31000 Toulouse*

In Japan: Please write to *Penguin Books Japan, Ishikiribashi Building, 2–5–4, Suido, Bunkyo-ku, Tokyo 112*

In Greece: Please write to *Penguin Hellas Ltd, Dimocritou 3, GR–106 71 Athens*

In South Africa: Please write to *Longman Penguin Southern Africa (Pty) Ltd, Private Bag X08, Bertsham 2013*

BY THE SAME AUTHORS

Hazell and the Three-Card Trick

A ton of hard-gotten greengages from a grieving widow and James Hazell was in business. Fluke it most certainly was, but Mrs Spencer's cheque was going to make him a Mayfair man. All he had to do was prove that the dear departed Mr Spencer was a murder victim and not a suicide. Which turned out to be about as simple as spotting aces in an iffy East End card school . . .

Hazell and the Menacing Jester

Moneybags Beevers and his weird little problem first cropped up on a wet London morning in May. Someone was menacing his pretty young wife, and the impressario needed class to run him to ground. James Hazell was yearning for a taste of the high life. And long overdue some expensive Bond Street shoes. All of which made him the perfect patsy for a rich man's dangerous game . . .

and

They Used to Play on Grass